All His Damned Mother's Sons

Tim Kirk

This book is dedicated to and inspired by the works & life of Josh Lawson
November 15, 1969 - August 10, 2020

All His Damned Mother's Sons by Tim Kirk

978-1-962702-04-1 Paperback
978-1-962702-05-8 Ebook

Copyright © 2025 Tim Kirk
Library of Congress Control Number: 2025938660

Cover artwork by Mark Givens and Tim Kirk
Layout and book design by Mark Givens
Graphics by Scott Kinsey
Author photo by Briar Kirk

First Pelekinesis Printing 2025

For information:
Pelekinesis, 112 Harvard Ave #65, Claremont, CA 91711 USA

www.pelekinesis.com

All His Damned Mother's Sons

by

Tim Kirk

"Elvis died the day he joined the army."
  - John Lennon

"Elvis Presley died in 1959…"
    - *Great Rock N' Roll Swindle*, The Sex Pistols

Contents

Prelude

Stuck On You

Smack dab in the middle of a country which had only recently been an enemy, the Friedberg base is an isolated island surrounded by people who speak a different language and are governed by a post-war bureaucracy that no one can fathom. Sergeant Folsom knows that the strict protocol of the military is the anchor that the men stationed here need and rely on.

And yet, here he is, wearing only three stripes yet riding high in his chariot, sitting in back like royalty, cruising among the high wire fences, zipping around the barracks, passing the munitions testing field, passing the fluttering flags, passing the signs with both English and German script, passing the marshalling men. At the wheel is his sharp-looking corporal, who is, to make matters worse, a big star back in the States.

The boy is the root of the problem. Folsom is pretty sure that he's the reason that the captain gave Folsom the jeep. To get rid of the boy. The captain claimed at the time that the arrangement made it hard to do his job, what with all the attention the corporal was drawing. Christ, who was he kidding? The captain never stepped outside without every medal and commendation pinned to his uniform, freshly buffed and shining, like he's in an Armistice parade. What a peacock!

The truth is that having the corporal for a driver brought all kinds of headaches. Not only were the Army press corps hounding him; the sergeant's superiors were watching. Watching for any sign of favoritism. Or, conversely, buckling down too hard. Folsom does not want to fuck up. All the commissioned men have heard the story of the officer back at Fort Hood who denied the corporal's request for leave when his mother was sick. The corporal threatened to go AWOL and finally got leave – but with only enough time for a hurried goodbye before she passed away. The scoop going around the mess hall is that this unlucky officer is sweating dirt at some shit outpost in the Philippines.

The jeep pulls up at the parade grounds just as the bugler plays the last note of Assembly. Folsom jumps out, a little too eager. Big and solid, moving quickly doesn't suit him.

"Join your platoon at munitions, Corporal."

"Yes sir!" The corporal responds with his melodic drawl and snaps a crisp salute. He drives towards the testing field and the pop-pop of small artillery.

Folsom breathes an unexpected sigh of relief. He knows it isn't the boy's fault. He's a likable sort. Unerringly polite. Neat as a pin. And, sure, there's something arresting about him. His smile shines like a beacon among the ever-present drab olive green.

Most of the men like him. When he was drafted, the Army offered him a cushy Secret Service gig, entertaining the troops, a couple of shows a month, stationed statewide. But he chose to do his duty just like the rest of the grunts. They like this about him. And they like writing home, especially the men with parents who dump on the corporal and his music, to tell them about all the swell things he has done. Like buying TVs for every barrack on the post and extra fatigues for the whole unit.

But some of them aren't buying his "I'm just an average Joe" attitude. They figure it's a bit, an act. They resent that he lives off base with his father and a bunch of friends from Memphis. Goes on dates with a pretty local girl. Poses for pictures. Real grunt work!

Samuels and his bunch in artillery seem to have it in for him in the worst way. 3rd Armored saw some hard fighting in WW2 and these grunts were there for all of it. They lost more than half of their unit and got a close-up view of them dying. Now, having fought hard to take cities like Friedberg, they resent the pussy-footing role of the Division. Maneuvers and "deterrent." Testing out-of-date ammo and explosives gets under their skin. As does a corporal like Elvis Presley.

The men of Company D hastily assemble on the parade ground, a hundred spines erect, two hundred shoulders squared, all eyes locked straight ahead.

Folsom considers them. All fresh. Three weeks ago they were state side at Fort Jackson in South Carolina. Now they are in Germany, at a base outside of a town they've never heard of and can't pronounce. As tough as they have been trained to look, Folsom knows many of them are lost, confused.

And they are all looking to him. The Sergeant. Strict but fair. Weathered and worldly. Keeper of the mysteries of military life, hell, even the mysteries of manhood. Folsom has learned to hide behind his stony expression and unwavering stare, but the whole thing makes him uncomfortable. Always has. Makes him tired.

He tries to imagine how Corporal Presley would feel in his shoes. He's stood before bigger crowds. That's what he does.

Folsom walks the front line of men, eyes piercing each as he passes. He positions himself before them, dead center.

"Parade rest!"

With a satisfying cadence of snaps and grunts, the men shift to a new position. Legs wide, rifles neatly tucked in their cradling arms.

Folsom scans the men, trying to feel what the corporal feels before a crowd. Power, he assumes. Energy. Yes, the attentive faces and riveted eyes would charge him up. The bigger the crowd, the bigger the charge. Folsom imagines the men multiplied by a thousand, living in the air, suspended by radio waves and TV transmissions.

His eyes are fixed on the horizon, picturing a mass of adoring humanity covering the world. He begins to sway slightly at the hips, the faintest trace of a wiggle, when he hears the explosion.

The jeep motors pell-mell from the artillery field, pursued by a column of smoke. The Corporal isn't driving. Folsom knows what has happened before the jeep can come to a stop.

Back in March, the fans had dubbed the day Presley was inducted as "Black Monday." Today was Thursday. The Sergeant wondered what'd they would call it.

"The World's Trusted Source for Reliable News"

The Hudson Tribune

Late Edition
Today, patchy morning fog sunny, high 55. Tonight, mo low 52. Tomorrow, a sho area, high 52. Weather ma SportsSunday, Page 12.

Copyright © 1959 Hudson Times

THURSDAY January 15th, 1959

Serving the greater New York metropolitan area

EPUBLICAN SEEK COMPROMISE

KEY STATES

epublican Political Groups Now Oppose Negotiation

By MIKE PROSETTI

Vith layoffs prompted by a tewide budget crisis getting the us, negotiations between the fied School District and the union represents its teachers have been on hold.

pause in the talks comes more n a year after the district and the ucation Association began gotiating a contract.

We would like to reach settlement ce so many neighboring districts e reached it, but right now layoffs the focus," the association's sident. "It's a matter of oritization."

The district has issued preliminary off notices to 305 teachers, nselors and school psychologists. addition, the board voted last nth to eliminate 28 probationary ching positions and accept the ignation of five employees.

puty Superintendent Joseph Davis d the various associations resenting teachers, administrators l non-teaching support workers all eed to postpone negotiations given budget issues.

The district faces about a $21 llion deficit next year as a result of rojected $16 billion state budget rtfall, proposed cuts to education nding totaling $4.4 billion tewide, and declining district ollment, Davis said.

t only does the district need to pen negotiations for 2007-08, but lso needs to start talks for 2008-09, said.

"The existing (budget crisis) pened to us and there was nothing yone could do but absorb the nch," Davis said. "And now we're ming out of a daze and we have to k at how we can work together."

The district and the union have a tory of stalemates and contentious gotiations over pay hikes, going k to the 1990s.

st May, the district and the teachers' ion settled on a 5 percent increase er a yearlong dispute. The sociation negotiated a 3.5 percent y raise in April 2006, after a adstill that lasted a year and quired a mediator.

Davis said concessions frequently ed in the private sector, such as lling back salary increases or quiring employees to contribute to ir health care costs, could be tried ease or prevent layoffs. Hedrick d that would be easier to do if the strict was more generous with its fers.

vis pointed to his measured and

continued of Page 10

ELVIS DEAD AT 24

By John Enbom

New York -- Elvis Presley, whose rock and roll records and appearances stirred millions of teenagers, was killed early morning on the munitions testing field of a US Army base in Friedberg, Germany, far from his hometown of Tupelo, Mississippi.

Presley was born Elvis Aaron Presley, January 8th, 1935, Tupelo, Mississippi to Gladys Love Smith and Vernon Presley.

The Presley family relocated to Memphis, Tennessee when Elvis was 13 years old. Elvis began his music career in 1956 with his number #1 hit, "Heartbreak Hotel." He toured the United States and appeared on television programs, including the Milton Berle Show, Steve Allen, and Ed Sullivan. His hits included "Hound Dog," "Don't Be Cruel", and "Any Way You Want Me."

On March 24th, Presley was drafted into the United States Army at Fort Chafee in Arkansas. He was allowed Emergency Leave in August to visit his mother in the hospital where she died two days later of heart disease.

Presley was stationed in West Germany in October, joining the 1st Medium Tank Battalion, 3rd Armored Division. He served there as an armor intelligence specialist. He also served as an officer's adjunct. His rank upon death was that of Corporal.

Details of Presley's death are unknown at this point. Sgt. Major Russ J. Martin, US Army Press Corp, expressed the Army's devotion to determine the veritiable elements behind the matter. "We do not know all of the particulars at this time. However, what we do know is that the incident was an accident. Moreover, we know, without any doubt, that no persons are to blame, certainly not the Corporal."

No word yet from family members. Vernon Presley, father of the deceased, is in seclusion. Fans around the world have shown their displays of sorrow for the loss of their icon. Somber marches have been spotted in Memphis, Dallas and New York City. Rock and roll radio stations have been playing "the King's" music around the clock in memoriam.

Colonel Tom Parker, Elvis' manager, has announced that a "studious investigation" is under way and that a

continued o, Page 4

Rebel's Advances Raise Funding and Tensions

By VICTORIA RUSKIN

About 14 miles from Baghdad International Airport, a mortar shell landed with a thud. A second followed, closer, and then a third struck across the Iraqi army's lines, as the Islamic State militants zeroed in on their target.

The volley of mortar fire outside the Baghdad suburb of Abu Ghraib this week was not unusual in itself; Islamic State fighters and the Iraqi army have regularly exchanged fire in this area for months. But now, officials worry that gains by the extremist group in neighboring will provide momentum for an assault on the outskirts of the capital.

Mortar shells fired by the Islamic State have already fallen in central Baghdad in recent weeks, and suicide bombings have picked up pace - a wave of blasts a killed at least 50 people in and around Baghdad on Thursday, local media reported. While the army is holding its ground around the capital's perimeter, Abu Ghraib is seen as a weak point, and sympathy for the radical fighters is growing here, residents say, because of the heavy-handed actions of Shiite militias.

Despite U.S. and allied airstrikes intended to crush them, the Sunni extremists have been steadily consolidating power in the majority-Sunni province to the west. Islamic State fighters continued to advance Thursday, closing in on the Anbar town of Amriyat al-Fallujah, one of the last in the province still controlled by the government. Local officials begged the government to send

continued of Page 10

Ambassador's Visit to China, Largely Ignored

By MIKE PROSETTI

U.S. Not Included in the "China Dream"

The primary purpose of this visit to Beijing, Qingdao, Xian, and Shanghai was to enhance understanding between our two countries and to promote collaboration between The Carter Center and our primary contacts in China. Recent polls indicate that only 10 percent of Chinese believe the United States can be trusted "a fair amount," and only 25 percent of Americans feel the same way about China. Many Chinese think the United States wants to change their political system and control the rapid growth of Chinese economic and political influence, while Americans are concerned about adverse trade imbalance and aggressive Chinese policies that create disharmony with Japan, the Philippines, South Korea, and Vietnam. The United States has political and military alliances with some of these countries.

There has been a tremendous surge in China's economic strength and worldwide diplomatic involvement during the past 35 years, since normalization of relations with the United States and simultaneous implementation of "reform and opening up" in China. This creates an inevitable competitive relationship between the two great powers. President Xi Jinping has become the most forceful Chinese leader since Deng Xiaoping, and some of his actions and statements have increased a sense of nationalism in China, with his emphasis on the "China dream." At the same time, President Obama has made statements to emphasize the renewed or increased commitment of the United States to an active role in Asia.

During this trip we focused on: a) finding areas of cooperation between our Center and friends in China regarding issues of mutual interest, especially regarding developing nations, b) educating young Chinese (future leaders) on how U.S.-Chinese relations might be improved, c) meeting with top policy makers and business leaders from both sides to engage in productive dialogue, and d) continuing our overall commitment to insuring sound and mutually respectful relations between China and the United States. Our new website, "U.S.-China Perception Monitor" is devoted to these same goals.

A few hours before we arrived in Beijing, the Ministry of Education instructed all the universities to refrain from sponsoring our events, which had been arranged many weeks ago. We began shifting the venues to hotels and attempted to learn the reason for this unprecedented departure from my previous treatment in China. However, this problem was quickly resolved, and may have been caused by a general concern about foreigners relating directly to students as well as a bureaucratic unease because of uncertainty regarding the massive anti-corruption drive. The two universities in Beijing and also in Shanghai went ahead with our previous arrangements, and we made the change easily in Xian Jiao Tong University.

All our public events were warm and cordial, and throughout our trip there were frequent celebrations of my upcoming 90th birthday, the 110th anniversary of Deng Xiaoping's birth, the 35th year of normal diplomatic

continued of Page 9

RE-TAPP OLD WEL OIL REN

NEW MONE

By NEILL DRISC

"We have ups, we ha all cycles through then again," said Coolidge, County commissio third-generation oil and g "What's happening with c coming."

How exactly to desc happening with oil now i River Basin and across subjective. It's hard to go Gillette without hearing oil here is "booming."

After nearly a quarte continual decline in oil Coolidge is hesitant to word but not by much.

"You know, that's a f said. "Are we booming? in the early stages of a bo certainly busy, all the ho booked, rental vacanc down. So yeah, maybe w

Coolidge and his f ridden the energy ro before, first with oil in th and mid-1980s, then recently with the coal-b boom. This time, he sa Campbell County and th for a long and exciting r

Aside from the mi percent vacancy rate for Gillette, hotels packed workers and the daily trucks crisscrossing Campbell and norther counties, the proof is in said Bruce Hinchey, pre Petroleum Association o

And the numbers are Oil production topped o nearly 130.5 million barr with 26.8 million of th from Campbell County highest on record with t Oil and Gas C Commission.

Production then went downward spiral. Sinc all-time low in 2009 produced 7.4 million ba production has exponentially.

In 2013, production was up to more than 13 m a 175 percent increase and is on pace to fill m million barrels this year.

Campbell County solidified itself as the c oil for the Cowboy Stat for 20.5 percent of Wyor production in 2013 ar percent for 2014 through

Those numbers "are c for the county, good fo Hinchey said. "The hote restaurants are full, th providing good paying work, but they're high- which means there's a lo

continued of P

egal Definition of Death Still Murky, Courts to Undertake Challenge

By JOHN WOLCOTT

It's not always easy to determine if meone is dead. Science, medicine, w or religions don't always offer nple guidance either.

But specific details around death do atter, and are not merely topics for ilosophical debate. For example, hen should someone be taken off e support? When is someone dead ough for organ donation?

The difficult topic of death will be

provided evidence for both sides.

Dr. Paul Fisher, head of Stanford Hospital's division of child neurology, argues she's dead.

Dr. Alan Shewmon, professor emeritus in neurology at UCLA, argues "she is an extremely disabled but very much alive teenage girl."

The McMath case and others raise longstanding questions about death for which the answers are evolving. When is someone dead?

"I know when one is dead, and

Water Conservationists and Big Business Team up on Environmental Stweardship

By CHAD RUBEL

Serious global challenges to the well-being of humanity require bold and innovative solutions. One example is the partnership between the World Wildlife Fund and Coca-Cola to address the dilemma of freshwater scarcity. At the beginning of the 21st century, the world faced a serious water crisis. About 97.5 percent of the world's water was in its oceans.

Of the remaining 2.5 percent that was fresh water, only about 30 percent was

marketing campaign, Arctic Home, to raise awareness about and provide funding for the polar bear and its habitat. In 2012, they agreed that the partnership would run through 2020.

Considering the expected world population of more than 9 billion by 2050, all of whom will depend on the same freshwater supply that exists today, new solutions are essential. As a public-private collaboration, this effort provides an opportunity to understand some of the characteristics and attributes of effective and

Man Charge Shooting H Patrol Office

A New York man i aggravated assault, ar action and unlawful us for shooting and woun police officer. Mo arrested Thursday nigh $250,000 bond. T happened early undercover officer Just and his partner sat in a Johnson was wounde

Chapter 1

Guitar Man

First day in the studio and it's not going well.

Billy knows what the band is thinking. He's off. Not off-key, just whacked-out, downtown, *flat*. Like, every note is a clunker. Lifeless. Uninspired. Real Joe Below.

He knows all that because he's been a session player himself, lugging his ax into a cramped studio for a day or a week to record someone else's songs then packing it up for the next gig. He's even played guitar with some of these cats. Gilby with the big bass was down at Crystal Sound last year with Bob Wills and his crew. Billy had played rhythm guitar on that one. He'd toured with John "Long John" Jackson when they were both briefly in Tex Ritter And His Texans, opening for Jimmy Wakely And His Saddle Pals. Long John's got the chops for real. He could hold a steady drum beat in the eye of a hurricane.

They had all cut their teeth in honky-tonks and ballrooms, playing in stripped-down four-man bands or eighteen-piece Western Swing ensembles. And when that wagon went downhill, they caught a ride on this new thing called Rock and Roll.

These guys knew him from the old days when he was just Billy.

Now he was Billy Clover, *The Next Big Thing. The Cowboy who rocks and rolls. The Singing Sensation with ruby hair, a flaming red curl dangling over his forehead.*

He'd only learned that he was that Billy three months ago. And, despite the interviews and photographs and contracts, he was still a guy holding a guitar. Feeling flat.

The musicians slouch, lean against their amps, smoke. White sound-buffering covers the grey concrete walls — the room looks like a padded cell. Billy slips on the cans and is about to count the combo off for another stab at "Big River Rockin'" when insistent knocking brings an urgent tempo to the languid room. The setting sun bursts through a distant window in the far back of the recording booth, silhouetting two women rapping their knuckles on the glass separating the band from the studio engineers hovering over their mixing board. Billy guesses one's a seamstress, judging by the pile of bright and shiny material she carries. The other is Sybil. Billy doesn't know what Sybil does but it's important.

Sybil enters talking. "Billy! Billy! Have we got a suit for you!" She snaps her bejeweled fingers at her assistant, red nails flashing. "Straight from the cutting table! Gorgeous! Gorgeous!" She descends like a tornado, big arms pointing and prodding. The assistant snaps gum and measures Billy's inseam. "If I only had your thighs," she sighs. Sequins pop. Needles fly. Billy has one arm in a sand colored Baracuta jacket with a zip front and rhinestone cuffs before he thinks to dismiss the band.

"Okay guys, take five."

Long John drops his sticks and rolls a smoke. He snickers behind his long whiskers, "take your time, Elvis."

Billy winces. And just like that, Sybil grabs his shoulders, locks him in an appraising gaze, hands on hips. "It all comes down to the portion of cowboy in balance with the portion of rock n roller," says Sybil for the millionth time.

"No," argues Billy, "it comes down to the boots and the hat." And he knows he's right. You can put as many sparkles on a black jacket as you like, but it'll still read Western or Rocker, no problem. In fact, the cowboy boots are okay, fancy embroidery or dangling chains, it's just a matter of degree. And they've brought a dozen for him to choose from.

But the hat...

"This is the one that makes it all work," Sibyl proclaims as she clamps the monstrosity on his head. It's got a tall crown and a wide brim like Autry used to wear, but the damn thing is made of leather, shiny black leather! "Sam will love it!"

And here is Big Sam himself! Filling the room like he fills his over-sized, but impeccably tailored, vest and coat. He swings wide a walking stick with a silver eagle handle, one of many affectations, and claps Billy on the back. "You're looking good, Billy! Looking sharp! A whole new world, my boy, a whole new world!"

"A whole new world, Big Sam."

Billy extends a hand, but the seamstress slaps it down. "Stay still, handsome," she scolds as she marks the sleeve with white chalk.

Big Sam waves some paper in Billy's face. "Hot off the presses. The Herald Examiner. Nationwide. An entire spread on Billy Clover, color photos and all. They are calling you the Crown Prince of Rock and Roll, which is mighty catchy. Come tomorrow morning, this will be on every doorstep, every newsstand, coast to coast."

Billy can't make out the text Sam is waving around but he knows the story. It's some fresh mutation of the tale of how Billy met Big Sam. It seems to grow more fantastical with each retelling.

It always goes something like this. Completely by accident, just a few months ago, Big Sam Thompkins happened to witness Billy Clover perform. The future star (and Crown Prince) was playing back-up that night for the house band in a little dinner joint in Santa Barbara. A two-night gig. In early stories, the place was called the "Backwater", then the "Shooting Star" but, as best as Billy can re-member, the sign above the door read "Abby's." Why Big Sam was in the house that night was a stroke of luck. No, not luck, provi-dence! He had a vacation house up there, just a short drive from Ventura where he managed an empire of industrial dishwashers, and he was hosting some guests for the weekend. Turns out his favorite restaurant was packed with a wedding party. So, Big Sam and his guests wandered into the Backwater/Shooting Star/Abby's just as the band was getting back from a break. Big Sam's big behind had barely touched the seat of his chair when his eyes fixed on the svelte, tall guitarist, swinging his flash Gibson Sunburst like a blazing comet, strutting across the stage. The band just played tired covers, "Mercury Blues," "Maybellene," "Blue Moon of Kentucky", but this kid's energy! His charisma! This voice, like an angel, a dirty angel, a very sexy angel. You'd have thought he was the only one on stage, that he was a superstar, that he was playing to a packed auditorium. No arguing about it, the kid had it. They talked after the show and, one newspaper concluded, "a new Star rose that night in the Western sky."

Which is grand, but not Big Sam's favorite. "Like Elvis reached down from Heaven and touched Billy Clover's guitar hand, pronouncing 'here is the new king.'" That's from the Times. This is what Big Sam loves to hear.

All this and he hasn't even cut one track.

Big Sam's booming voice fills the studio. "You got everything you need? Studio okay?"

"It's jake, Sam."

"It should be. It's the best damn studio in LA, they tell me. And it's costing me a mint." He claps his hands. "Let's hear you guys play something! Blow me down!"

Billy straps his guitar over his stiff new clothes. The sleeves are tight. He flexes his fingers and counts it off. "1, 2, 3, 4."

"I can't stop lookin' in the mirror, shakin' all the time, all I keep seeing is twisting double-time. Twistin' twins, twisting twins..."

"Whoa! Hold up. Hold it up!" Big Sam's eyes are wide and white against his flushed face.

As the band winds down and music collapses around him, Billy feels it again. Off. He's never really put a name on it before, but it is a familiar feeling. Off. It had something to do with recording studios — he had felt it before, every time he stepped into a studio. It just never mattered before. Back then, he was always backing someone else up. Playing their songs. It wasn't his record. Energy and charisma and all that was not what was expected of him.

But it was now.

Suddenly, two men in suits appear. They huddle with Big Sam and Sybil. After a long, whispered conference, Big Sam lays a heavy hand on Billy's arm, steering him away from the others.

He lowers his voice. "There's something missing here, boy."

Billy sighs. "I know."

"You've got a lot of responsibility riding on those shoulders of yours. My money, my time, the whole machine we've put together." He waves his hand, encompassing the room and its occupants. "But this is big. Bigger than all that."

Billy can swear Big Sam has dollars floating in his eyeballs.

"Elvis had his shot, rest in peace, but now we got you. You're something the world has never seen, Billy. A man with super star pizzazz bringing a big band country style to rock and roll. How can you lose? You'll be bigger than Elvis ever was!"

Of course, Big Sam wasn't the only one with a dream. There were plenty of impresarios pushing their Next Big Thing. Even Tom Parker was in on the game, the Colonel himself.

Who could resist? Elvis' death had been big news and still was, nine months later. Colonel Parker did it up big. He somehow arranged for the King's body to be flown back from Germany with all the military pomp that the Army could summon – color guards, 21 gun salutes, a coffin covered with the flag, even a full military band playing somber versions of Elvis' hits. Then the train trip from

New York to Memphis, with whistle stops at every city, village or hamlet along the way. Long, long lines of mourners placed flowers on the coffin, though Billy couldn't imagine what was left of Elvis' body in there – an explosion like the one at Friedberg makes a hell of a hole in a guy.

The papers compared his Graceland funeral to Eisenhower's inauguration, but everybody knew that Ike lost out to the King big-time.

The first posthumous disc came out that very day, mostly a backlog of songs Elvis laid down before shipping out. For a while, his music was everywhere, on the radio, on TV – it was like he never left. The Colonel quickly launched a new singer playing Elvis' unrecorded material, 'Stuck on You' and 'Are You Lonesome Tonight,' and another guy filling the role in *G.I. Blues* Elvis was slated to play after his service. Neither really took.

And then nothing. Where was the Colonel? What happened to his new stars? Nothing.

And that's when people realized that Elvis was really dead. And some of those people saw a vacuum. People with vision and money on the mind. People like Big Sam.

"It's about Western Swing, Billy. The best damn music this country ever brought into being. And it never got as big as it could have been, as big as the world needs. It had the momentum of a charging locomotive in the forties, with the movies and the radio and the fans! But it just petered out in the fifties. Why? Cuz Gene Autry got old. Cuz Bob Wills was too goofy. Cuz Spade Cooley was a nut. The music never had the superstar it deserved. Rock and Roll had Elvis Presley. God bless his soul. Who did we have? No one. Not until now! Not until Billy Clover!"

These words echo in the now empty studio, just the two of them.

"And yet..." Big Sam takes a deep breath and blows it out long and slow. "Something's missing."

Hell yeah, something was missing. Billy has heard this speech many times and it still inspires and everything, but the magical merger of big band Western Swing with Rock and Roll was just talk. There is still the matter of songs. And that's all on him.

"Fiddle!" blurts Billy.

"What's that?"

"I gotta have a fiddle player."

"Well, boy, I got you Tobin there. He's the best. They all say that he's the best."

Feeling like he was drowning, Billy desperately treads water, elaborating. "It's just the way I'm hearing these songs, Sam. I need Walter Rogers. Old Walt is the best fiddler you ever heard." He puts on his best charm, hiding his growing panic. "I'm telling you, Old Walt is the best since Cain brained Abel, since Adam ate the apple. He is a force of nature, Sam."

Big Sam studies Billy for a beat, his conviction, his sparkling eyes, his perfect hair. "This Walt... he's what's missing?"

"Yes, sir, he is."

Sam sighs. "Okay. You round him up. We'll break for dinner and pick back up at eight. Eight sharp."

*   *   *   *   *

Western Avenue is a sea of umbrellas. Clubs and restaurants fill the block. The rain-slick sidewalks are packed with people out on the town for dinner and some music. Mostly sharp-dressed black folks. Add a dash of white A-listers pouring from long limos into packed nightclubs, fresh from Chasen's or a masquerade party in the hills. A smattering of hoodlums, some sketchy, some happy and drunk. Hustlers and pimps. A cold wind whips the rain. Billy pulls up his collar and keeps his hand on his wallet, frantically winding his way through the crowds, eyeing each passerby, looking in every doorway, down every alley.

He turns a corner onto the broader Jefferson, then into a dark, thin alley the locals call 'Dump Street'. He ducks around the spewing gutters of filthy brick buildings. The alley is littered with flop houses. Billy knows them well. He figures he's crashed at all of them, one time or another, often bunking with Walter.

Billy and Walter met at Riverside Rancho, the hopping roadhouse out near Griffith Park. It was the place to be if you liked Western music that's got that swing. The joint had giant dance floors, down home Oklahoma cooking, and working folks dressed to the nines seven nights a week. It was 1949. Billy was just 12 but he got the gig anyway, maybe because he was tall for his age, maybe because he grew a wispy mustache (long gone), maybe because they heard him play his busted-up guitar and that was that.

Every night at Riverside Rancho was New Years Eve. The folk who worked there were a tight group. There was Kate, a giantess of a woman, who managed the joint, booked the acts and did just about everything else. Pretty Maddie was sweet sixteen and led a cadre of fresh-faced gals carrying trays filled with never-ending beer steins. Nathan ran the bar in his trademark blue overalls.

Maybe it was more like perpetual Thanksgiving. They were family, but someone else's family. They were all Okies who were blown away from home by the Dust Bowl. They had dared the phalanx of club-wielding sheriffs at the Arizona border and made a new home for themselves in the Northeast corner of Los Angeles. Billy's family was from Oklahoma as well, but the winds off the prairies had blown them in a different direction and they had landed in Sulphur Springs, up near Fresno. Grandpa did some picking in the fields. Dad did some drinking.

His childhood home was a tiny place on a large tract near the edge of town. Downtown was bustling for about a minute and then that passed. An old shed sat rotting out back, a long walk into the woods, near a stinking pond. It was a crazy misshapen size, and it didn't make any sense to young Billy. What was it doing all the way out there? And right next to that pond that stank of death, like a thousand fish died and sank to the shallow bottom of its murky waters. Billy collected bottles and created glass structures in the shed. Forts and missiles and one time even a giant dog. He picked up some of his building material by the side of the road on the walk home from school. But mostly he relied on the bottles that his dad tossed in a pile out back of his bedroom window. At least twice a year that supply would suddenly dry up, and this seemed to coincide with an increased family attendance at Sulphur Springs First Baptist.

When that happened, Billy had to really search for his bottles. This led him to the train tracks and the treasure trove of whiskey bottles there. That's where he met the hobos who taught him to play guitar.

The hobos also taught him how to jump a train, which came in handy when he was 12. He remembers what happened at the little house near the lake, the one in Bakersfield where his father sent him. Where the loons screamed at night. A memory he tries not to think about.

A hooker in an electric blue nylon raincoat beckons from a nearby stoop, giving Billy a welcome distraction from his thoughts. "See something you like, Cowboy?" She performs a near perfect pirouette on silver-toed heels, shaking her ass as a grand finale.

Billy keeps rushing, saying, "naw," and then "no offense, ma'am," tipping his four-gallon hat, discovering that the disgrace to humanity is still up there. He chucks the damn cowboy hat into the sewer.

"None taken, sugar. And aren't you such a polite boy. And awful cute."

Billy walks backwards, throwing a question down the block. "You seen Walter?"

"Walter? Who's Walter?"

"Never mind."

He spins on his heels, eyes up, on the trail. Walter landed in the Riverside Rancho by a different route. After the war, he headed to LA from somewhere way up north where it was always cold. The GI bill promised every former soldier a brand-new house for cheap, and Walter decided to take them up on it. He wasn't the only one. Houses were going up blocks at a time, in new towns called Lakewood or Panorama city. There was still a backlog, so the Army put Walter and the rest of the wait-listers up in Rodger Young Village, the temporary site of hundreds of Quonset huts on the old airfield in Griffith Park, just a short walk from the Rancho. Billy often crashed there with him and his wife. When Walter's number came up in the house lottery, he and the wife were through, and Walter was past the whole "home ownership trap".

Walter is old enough to be Billy's dad, but he's never asked a single thing about Billy's past and Billy appreciates it. They get along that way, always have. When the Rancho got closed down by the police, this time for good, Billy and Walter picked up short gigs with other outfits, sometimes playing in the same bands, sometimes not. They appeared as members of a quartet backing up Smiley Burnette's comic antics in a few Durango Kid films until they stopped making those.

Billy passes the Shimmy Shack, the Hotspot and the Baby Bijou. Music pours from each open door, giving Billy a skip in his step. The music, the people, the cool rain – it all clears his mind and pumps up his mood. This is candy for our man.

A crowd clogs the sidewalk ahead, forming around an impromptu duo playing in a dry alcove under an archway – two young black kids , snare drum and trumpet. Billy jumps over the rushing gutter and onto the black asphalt street, picking up speed and stepping in time with the beat. Damn, that trumpet can blow.

The kid is so small, his skinny arms don't seem like they could hold the golden trumpet in his hands. But he can play. Billy spots right away the kid's hero behind every dazzling race through phrases, the serpentine rhythms turned on a dime. The great Dizzy Gillespie. The crowd is eating it up.

A chirp interrupts the melody as a black and white patrol car pulls up alongside Billy and keeps pace. The uniformed cop behind the wheel leans out the window. Rain streams off his peaked hat.

"Keeping out of trouble, Billy?"

Billy flashes a smile but does not slow. "Mostly trying to fight off the raindrops, officer."

"You're losing that battle," chuckles the cop's partner. He flicks his cigarette into the pouring rain. "A friend wants to say hello."

The car accelerates. The back window rolls down revealing a heavy man in a dapper suit with soup stains on both lapels.

"So they finally got you, Marcus."

"Fair and square, Billy," chortles the chubby man with the hairless face. Heavy set eyes with startlingly bright blue eyes. "Minors at the club again. I haven't the *faintest* idea how that happens." Appreciative guffaws from the front seats. "Aw," continues Marcus, "these are good boys. They got to do this every so often."

"You comfortable back there, Mr. Rydell?"

"Can't complain, boys." He shows Billy his two free hands. "No cuffs. No fuss. A very leisurely drive. I called my lawyer back at the club. At this pace, he'll probably get to the station before they can book me."

"Since you're in a such a good mood, feel like giving me the scratch you owe me for the Lester Rhodes gig?"

"Everyone knows Rudy Dean plays guitar in Lester's band. And since when do you play jazz?"

"I've been sitting in with these cats since I was big enough to slip in the back door. Besides, Rudy hocked his guitar, and I play any gig that pays." Billy protests. "C'mon, Marcus. You couldn't miss me. I was several shades paler than the rest of the band."

"I'm remembering now. The white kid hiding in the back."

"Lester and his gang are incredible. It's tough to keep up but the places they take you. What a ride – whoo!"

Marcus Rydell makes a dumb show of pulling out the sleeves of his suit pockets. Empty. "I can't give what I don't have. This nightclub bizness is for the birds. Look at me, just 30 and hairs falling out everywhere." He's not lying. Receding hair and a baby face – it's a strange look. "You know me, Billy. I'll book any band, any kind of music, black or white, as long as they cook. One night the place is packed and the next it's empty-ville."

"That's swell. Where's my money?"

"I'm done, Billy. I'm closing the Flame. Enough with that nonsense. I'm going to concentrate on the one thing that's sure money – whores! Then it's the easy street for me. Come and see me then."

A red cherry on top of the patrol car flashes and the traffic ahead makes way. The cop behind the wheel gives Billy a parting salute.

"Stay straight, kid."

"That's the plan, officer."

"If you change your plan," shouts Marcus as he disappears down the street, "you got my number. I dig your style, Billy. I'd like to see your dark side. See the Irish in you."

Seems to Billy that there is always someone telling him what to do these days. That's what he likes about Walter. No sermons.

Turning back onto Western Avenue, Billy plunges into the main drag. The Club Oasis towers over the avenue, lines of Imperials and Coup De Villes for miles, snazzy valets holding bright red parasols, decked-out cats swaggering their way into the club to hear Miles Davis and his sound. Smaller clubs buzz like bees around the Oasis, spilling music onto the street — a cacophony of different styles — bebop, cool jazz, swing, rhythm and blues, even a South Seas vibe over at Waikiki's – all competing for Billy's attention. His ears perk up and he follows one melody through the morass to the Short Stop Dance Hall. He waves at a familiar bouncer outside the alley door (Marty? Mickey?) and soon finds himself in front of the stage, where Walter is tearing the roof off with his wild fiddle.

Walter looks a lot older than the last time Billy saw him. And his fiddling is not the tsunami it once was. It's massive, it's accomplished, but Billy has to admit to himself that the rail thin fiddler has slowed some. Regardless, the room is pulsating. Partners spin around the crowded dance floor, a massive shared heartbeat in sync with wild drums and the bow prancing up and down Walter's fiddle.

This is a damn big band for a space this size. Lots of strings – cello, another fiddler besides Walter – plus piano, drums, three tenor saxophones, stand-up bass and a steel guitar. Billy smiles. It reminds him of the glory days back at Riverside Rancho.

He waves Walter to the side of the stage. Still playing, Walter smiles his toothy smile and shouts above the band. "Billy Clover hisself!" Billy shouts back, about the studio and the gig and the need for Walter and his fiddle, but Walter just cups a hand to his ear and shakes his head. Billy leans closer. That is his mistake. Walter has his hands now and pulls him onstage.

A couple of guys in the band smile and someone lets loose with a triumphant whoop! A guitar is placed around his neck and, before he knows it, Billy is playing.

The effect is instantaneous. The music of the band surges through him and collects in his fingers. The guitar sings. Fingers zing. The crowd sings back. Billy can't make out their features in the shadowy room, just a surging mass of excitement. He feels so full of electricity; he might just explode. He dances with his guitar, covering the stage, owning it. Tossing rock and roll into the western vibe, a jubilant virus coursing through the melody, ripping it up, tearing it up. The world is a whirling storm and he's right in the center of it.

He is not off. He is far, far, far from off!

The lead sax steps center stage, and the band takes a break. This is a new thing for a western ensemble – a sax solo. Billy huddles with Walter by the drum stand.

"What time is it?! What time?!"

Walter holds up ten fingers. Now it's Billy's turn to grab Walter and pull him off the stage.

*   *   *   *   *

Billy crashes into the studio, Walter right on his tail. It's nearly midnight. The band members droop in various corners.

Big Sam angrily stabs out a cigarette in a tray full of butts. "Where the hell have you been?!"

Billy only straps on his guitar and counts off a fast tempo. "1,2,3,4!" He shakes the rain from his hair and launches into something new, something upbeat and jumping. His guitar is once again alive in his hands.

Walter picks up the tune and joins in. Slowly, the rest of the band follows.

"The sun is set. The day is done. The stars are out and it's quitting time. So light that fire and kick up your boots! Let's show this night what it's like swing and what it's like to rock!"

Billy's energy is contagious. 18 karat! "Break it down," he shouts. Pretty soon, the whole band is flying, and the music is bouncing off the walls.

Big Sam beams. There's no guessing involved. This jam is in the pocket.

*   *   *   *   *

The two old friends pass a bottle on a park bench, watching a murky sun peek out from beneath a hazy horizon. They've played until dawn, cutting four singles and woodshedding two more.

"You know who Sam reminds me of? Smiley Burnette himself."

Walter makes a drunken shushing sound. "I doubt he'd like the comparison much."

"Remember when we were doing that looney bird number out at Colombia Ranch? On one of the Durango Kid flicks, 'West of Someplace' or 'South of Someplace.'"

"The one where Smiley was running around with a big net trying to catch some imaginary bird?"

"Yeah, he's hilarious. At the end, Smiley was supposed to put the net over one of us in the band and the guy gives a goofy look like he belongs in a nut house."

Walter sticks out his tongue and bugs his eyes. "Like this?"

"Yeah, they gave it to Lester."

"Lester was hell on a mandolin."

"I'll drink to that."

Billy takes a long pull on the bottle and passes it Walter's way. "Well, you did it, Walter. You're my magic charm."

"No, Billy. It weren't me." He takes the bottle from Billy and wipes the mouth. "You got what it takes."

"Now don't go calling me Elvis."

"I'm being truthful. You and E share something. Something hungry on the inside but still beautiful on the out. Could take you places." He paused. "I wouldn't want to die like that, though."

"Death comes to all of us."

"Yeah, but it didn't seem like Death could catch ol' Elvis. Folk loved him so much. Sad that all that love couldn't save him. Maybe an equal amount hate out there, maybe less, but strong."

"You're not going conspiracy talking on me, are ya?"

"How else you figure? An explosion, a mistake? I don't think so. Somebody wanted him dead."

"I don't buy it."

"You buy heroic Corporal Presley jumping on a wayward mortar to save his whole platoon?" Walter spits.

"Crazier things have happened."

"Crazy like a country boy from Sulphur Springs becoming a superstar?"

"You're talking like Big Sam."

"Maybe he's got a crystal ball."

"For sure he's got a whip and a chain. He's gonna expect another barnburner of a session like last night. And I don't got it in me."

Walter worries a stain on his shirt, gives it a pensive look. "You ever play much out in Colorado?"

"Naw. Furthest east I ever got was Albuquerque. "

"I did some fall gigs up in the Rockies with Bill Monroe and his crew at some resort there. They put the band up out by the river. Colder than you can imagine. There were a bunch of Indians that lived there. We all got friendly, and they ended up inviting me to their sweat lodge one night. The craziest thing. You huddle in this teepee with a pile of red-hot rocks and just sweat like the living hell. Outside, there's piles of snow but you are burning up in there.

When you get about as red as the devil himself, then you run outside and jump in one of those snow piles. Just dive right in there. It's the wildest feeling, I cannot get close to explaining it."

He passes Billy the bottle, but holds on to it, fixing Billy with a heavy look. "That's you, boy. You get all keyed up on stage, like you to pop, then dive right into the studio. It creates magic."

"Something changes me, Walter. Something about being up there. It's like everything all at once, a good meal, a beer or three, and sex. Sex is up there too. It's like church."

Walter laughs. "The church of Riverside Rancho."

"It's a thrill, I admit."

"A miracle for sure. But not a church miracle. Maybe it comes from the other end of things. It's dangerous, Billy. That's part of its power."

A clock tower in the park strikes eight. "Damn," says Billy, "we got to get back." He blanches. "I'm dragging, Walter. The magic is gone. I need another jolt."

"Don't snap your cap. I can fix it, Billy."

"Where are you gonna find a show this time of the morning?"

"Naw. Watch this." Walt takes the bottle, carefully screws the cap back on, stands and chucks it across the park. The bottle hits a lounging patrol cop, hits him square in the head. His hat flies off, the copper spins, wiping blood and exuding rage.

"Shit, what did you do, Walter?"

"Run!" yells Walter and they both do.

They hit the street just as a streetlight changes, so they duck and dodge right through traffic, a Lincoln's brakes squealing, bumper brushing their butts. The sidewalks are clear so they speed up, wheezing and coughing. The boy in blue is right behind them and closing fast.

As they turn the corner onto Sunset Boulevard, Walter trips and goes down. He waves Billy on.

"Go! Go!"

Arms pumping, hair flying, lungs about to burst, Billy crashes into the studio. He grabs the mic. He shouts.

"And 1, 2, 3, 4!"

Chapter 2

Heartbreak Hotel

The rattlesnake is fast asleep. It's nice and warm under that rock. So, when the rock topples, the snake isn't ready. Before it can coil and strike, or even rattle, Alvin has grabbed it by its scaly hide and swung it high in the air.

All in all, he thinks, catching a rattler is the easy part. The snake arcs through the air and strikes the hard earth. Alvin's steel-toed work boot cracks the little skull like the shell on a hardboiled egg.

It's the next part that separates people into one group or the other. As he grips the layered leather handle of his knife, Alvin divides up the folks he's met in his seventeen years on earth. Could they or couldn't they? His exquisitely curved eyebrows arch as he considers the equation, his brown eyes dreamily drifting upwards. The sturdy blade slides into the snake just below the jaw. Probably his old man could. Maybe those old coots on the rodeo circuit, not all of them, not the riders, maybe the wranglers.

With a sharp jerk, he severs the head. Small specks of blood spot his jacket. He wipes the black leather clean with a starched white handkerchief. None of the girls. Not a one. No disrespect. Just ain't their nature.

He pins the twitching carcass to a rock between fist and foot. The blade begins its long journey down the length of the snake, splitting the skin and the tender flesh beneath.

What about the hard boys back at the Castle? Maybe one or two – maybe Rick or Carl or that big black cat he only saw in the yard, the one they called Bumpy.

He lays the split snake next to the others on a flat stone near the river, to dry in the last rays of the day. That makes twelve. He kneels and washes his hands in the swift whitewater. He catches his reflection in a still eddy. He presses a stray lock of jet-black hair back into place and crosses Rick off the list. And he wouldn't swear that Carl or Bumpy could cut up twelve snakes on one lazy summer day, not for profit or nothing, just for something to do. No, he wouldn't swear to it, not before a judge or nothing.

Looming above this rocky riverbed with its fast-moving and treacherous-looking water, is fifteen floors of casino. The Mapes has an imposing decor and pointed pinnacles. So far, it's the biggest and the best in Reno. Alvin can see the neon blinking on all along Virginia Street, outlining the casinos fashioned on themes of silver mining or the majesty of the Sierras. Where the strip ends, so does the neon, but it still casts its glow over the motels and shops way down that way.

"I found one! There's one over here!" Mika's shirt is dirty and his shorts are third generation hand-me-downs. That's the way the kids on the reservation dress.

"Is it a big one, Mika? I don't have time for no gutter snakes."

"Looks pretty big, Alvin." He stretches his arms to show how big. He's about 10 years old.

They both freeze at the sound of a car's engine. Mika ducks behind some rocks and Alvin climbs up onto the highest boulder overlooking the water.

A cherry blue Chrysler bounces over the rough dirt road followed by a dust trail. Alvin recognizes the occupants and adds two more names to his list. Mitchell and Loren. Couldn't. Couldn't.

Feigning boredom, Alvin combs his greased hair straight back from his forehead. In his black jeans, white t-shirt and leather jacket, he looks just as cool as he plans on looking. He sings low under his breath, *"ya ain't nuthin but a hound dog, crying all the time..."*

"Alvin! Come down here. We want to talk to you."

"...ya ain't never caught a rabbit, and ya ain't no friend of mine..."

Mitch has squinty eyes and a freckled face. He wears his varsity football jersey even though school has been out for 3 weeks. He's a foot shorter than Alvin because that's the way God saw fit to make him, just like his tiny mother often says to his tiny dad. "We've been driving up and down Virginia Street looking for your sorry ass."

"What the hell you looking 'round there for, Mitchell. You know I don't like throwing my money away. Unless, of course, Loren's mother is open for business."

Loren plays linebacker. He's nearly as big as Alvin, but not as lean. He sports a crew-cut just like Mitch's. "Go screw, Alvin."

"Like I was saying."

"How you stand the heat out here? You ever take off that leather jacket?"

"No sir. Not since January 15th. You dig?" Alvin crosses himself.

"God bless the King?"

"You got that right."

"You're the most, Alvin." Loren hauls a cooler from the back seat. He fishes out a bottle. "Beer?"

"Thank you, Loren, you always were a good sport."

Alvin catches the Schlitz and pulls an opener from his back pocket. Mika slinks up, standing close to Alvin. "You boys know Mika?"

Mitch sneers. "Thought his name was Tonto."

"That's a good one, Mitch. Say, can you lend me a few bucks?"

Mitch takes out his wallet. Alvin grabs it from his hands. "Hey!"

"Just a loan." He counts out ten dollars and hands them to Mika.

"Wipe me out why don't you?"

The kid beams. Alvin shrugs. "You want a beer too?" Mika nods. Alvin musses his hair. "No beer for you, kid. Get out of here!" Mika dutifully takes off, skipping across the rocks along the river. "What can I do? I tell the little guy to do something, and he does it." The kid waves and disappears. Alvin darkens. "They got it tough at the reservation."

Mitch swallows some beer. "So we've been doing some drinking. Drinking and thinking and driving around looking for you."

Loren pipes up. "We got a proposition for you, Alvin. There's money in it."

Alvin just says, "crazy."

Mitch tosses Loren the Chrysler's keys. "I'll ride with Alvin, fill him in on the whole she-bang. You follow in the Chrysler. And don't mess it up. That thing is brand new and my dad doesn't know I borrowed it from the lot."

A whistle. Mika is dancing atop a rock, brandishing a beer over his head. Alvin chuckles.

"That little rat. He snaked a beer."

*　*　*　*　*

The old shocks on the Studebaker truck squeak and complain as Alvin steers it down the bumpy dirt road. It's making out better than the Chrysler behind him. Alvin hates to think what the undercarriage looks like.

The wheels hit the asphalt of the highway and Alvin punches the gas. The snakes slide around in the bed of the truck. A couple end up behind a box of his dad's shit. The truck's registration is in his dad's name, Rusty Pepper, but his dad doesn't have much use for it since a steer stomped on his stomach last July up at the rodeo there in Quincy. He won the medal anyway and traded it for a roll of morphine that he chewed up the first chance he got after realizing his legs didn't work no more. Since then, Alvin's mom has been dating a string of rodeo fools, so he doesn't see her too much.

"Here's the pitch, Alvin. My father knows all the big shots around here. Hell, he sells them all their Caddies. Turns out an associate of my father's happens to be looking for a little help and you're the swinging dick that came to mind. This fellow has sway. And he's looking to expand that sway. He's got some interest in a little piece of land out where the 395 hooks up with the Mount Rose highway. Now, it's a big spread and he owns the place and nobody can say nothing about that. Except there is some friction out there. A problem. You know what I mean?"

"I haven't a fucking clue."

"Those old Cozy Pines tourist cabins. You know the place — boarded up old cottages where people used to go to after driving up from L.A., a place to crash before they went on into to Reno to get hitched or get split or blow their wads."

"I can picture that."

"Seems a bunch of Basque bastards are squatting out there. They made their way down from Winnemucca and now they're working for some sheep ranch out in Minden."

"And these folks don't want to leave?"

"Nope." Mitch pops another beer and takes a big gulp.

Alvin watches the Chrysler in the rearview as it struggles to keep up. He considers his future. High school is over, and he sees his former schoolmates looking around and sizing up their options. He too finds himself wondering now and then what employment awaits him. Despite a dad who's a doped-up cripple, and a part-time mom, Alvin's had it pretty easy. He never had to sweat the grades and, as far as he can figure, he's God's gift to women. Also, the various low-lifes on the rodeo and in the bars always liked him. More times than he can count, some deeply sick drunk would give

Alvin his last buck, just because he got a kick out of the kid with his greaser get-up and his Elvis charm.

For a long time, Elvis cast a light on life's path. Alvin figured that if he could be just half as cool as Elvis, things would all fall into place.

But since Elvis' death, he's been left wondering where he was headed. His charm with high school girls and rodeo bums doesn't point to an obvious profession. He has skills but nothing extraordinary. Except for that one thing. He doesn't know a name for it, but he has a feeling it might make him different. It's something that most folks don't have. It's related to the things he can do with snakes, what he feels when he does those things or, actually, what he *doesn't* feel.

It's not quite that, and the skill has yet to be tested, but he knows, in a warm place deep inside him, that it is true – that he is special.

"So, who is this fella, this big shot?"

"This is Reno, Alvin. He's big, he's in the business, and he don't fool around. What do you think?"

"Roger Bolles."

"Then you know the score. Bolles will *return the favor*! He will *set us up!*"

"What's the favor?"

Mitch lowers his voice to a conspiratorial whisper. "He's got a sweet deal in mind for that land out there by Cozy Pines. It's a hotel. The biggest one yet. The Taj Mahal of casinos, but these sheepherders are standing between him and this sweet deal."

"These creeps are an obstacle, huh? And we make like a bulldozer and clear them away?"

"Bolles will be beholden to us, big time! We'll have it made in the shade!"

Something starts to glow in Alvin's warm place. He feels light-headed and everything he sees and hears sort of slips off somewhere.

"We'll have the run of the place. Everything comped. VIP treatment."

Alvin comes back from his dreamy place. "Here's my answer. I'll join you boys on this little adventure, and I'll help this fella remove his obstacles. Like Elvis said, 'Ambition is a dream with a V-8 engine.' But I ain't going to do nothing just for some pie in the sky BS. You guys can dream your little dreams all you want – how big your suites are gonna be, how many showgirls you can screw. Me? After we're done, I'm walking straight into the boss' office. Mr. Roger Bolles will know my name."

Mitch is laughing and clapping. Maybe he's celebrating too much but Alvin doesn't notice. He's heading back inside his head. He finds it there waiting – the path before him, his way through life. He contemplates how neatly this new opportunity fits with his ideas, what some might call his "career objectives." To hook up with a powerful fella and do the shit that he won't, or can't, do. That's where Alvin's special skill comes in. His ability to handle certain things.

Sure, Bolles is rich and he's powerful. But he's *Reno* rich and powerful. Alvin figures he can hitch himself to this guy's star for a while and get some work experience and some money and some pussy. And then, when it's time, he can move on up to a bigger guy with a brighter star.

Alvin imagines a ladder heading upwards, with more money and better pussy on every rung. A ladder headed all the way to pussy heaven.

Descending from the clouds, he sees Mitch's scheming and drunk-red face before him. And he realizes that this guy is, in fact, the first rung.

"So you're in, Alvin?"

"Not much going on tonight anyway. *King Creole* has been playing over at the Sagebrush for a month now." He spits. "What a shame. That boy could dance."

* * * * *

Tom Elliot steers his brother's red Ford Crestline sedan down the frontage road, driving with one hand and sipping a warm can of Schmidt with the other. He had to close up at the A&W so he's late to the party and trying to catch up with his pals' buzz. There is something delicate about Tom, despite his football physique. He takes a large gulp of beer and nearly gags. He's new to this drinking thing.

A second-hand acoustic guitar bounces on the seat beside him, strings humming with the vibrations of the sedan. Tom picks up the accidental tune and hums along.

The casino lights are over the horizon and it's dark. The Sierra crests are to the west and the Paramint Hills to the east. Alpine is everywhere. It's an inspiring sight, sort of melancholy, thinks Tom, wondering if some lyrics might come to him.

Instead, his favorite song pops into his head.

Tell your story
Roll the truth around in your head
Bound for Glory
Dreamin' in a cowboy song
I feel I'm bound for glory

"Dreamin' in a cowboy song," he repeats.

Daisy turned him on to this song. His cousin is three years older and already living on her own up there in San Francisco. When she visits, she brings a bunch of records. He pictures her now, sitting on the living room carpet, her long legs spread around the Victrola on the floor, singing along. Those freckled legs...

Later, at night, they'd huddle in his room, and she'd read aloud. She'd lay some poetry on him, stuff from the poets in San Francisco, the Beats they called themselves. He liked the heavy stuff. She turned him on to some cat named Michael McClure.

> *I smile to myself, I know*
> *all that there is to know, I see all there*
> *is to feel. I am friendly with the ache*
> *in my belly. The answer*
> *to love is my voice.*

Daisy says he was high when he wrote it. Tom wonders what that's like. Shifting gears as the road ahead climbs, Tom rubs the rough corduroy of his red pants. His secret freak flag.

He wants to write stuff like that. Stuff that makes him feel. She reads him Keats and, boy, that guy can write. It burns him up inside, just sets his soul on fire.

> *Can death be sleep,*
> *while life is but a dream,*
> *and scenes of bliss pass as*
> *a phantom by?*

Waking from his reverie, he spots the sign at the last minute and swerves onto the gravel road towards Cozy Pines Cabins.

Just last week, his brother mounted a patrol light to the car's door. Tom aims its beam on a row of deserted cottages. Doors and windows boarded up, the small cabins are overgrown with sagebrush and wild blackberries. The spotlight reaches the last cottage. Address numbers dangle uselessly from the door.

Up ahead he sees the Chrysler and Alvin's old Studebaker. He kills the engine.

"Hey fellas. I hope you saved me some beer. Mr. Jenkins is a real stickler on punch out time."

Mitch and Loren lean against the truck, breathing hard. Mitch gulps air. "Holy shit! You should have seen it. It was insane! Them sheepfuckers were all asleep. We busted in and Alvin smashed a chair against the wall. Splinters everywhere! Man, those guys just bolted."

"Scared shitless!" adds Loren.

"Where's Alvin?"

"He took off after one of them."

Tom aims his beam into the dark space past the cabins. Alvin raises a bloody hand against the light. "Cut that shit off!" He walks past the boys to his truck. "Getting a little shaggy there, aren't ya, Tom."

"Oh, letting it grow a little. Something new for the summer, you know?"

"Where's the letterman jacket? Ain't that you boys' uniform?"

"Got a new uniform now, Alvin. A&W fry cook, officer first class reporting for duty." Tom's laugh dies as Alvin pulls off his shirt. It's covered in blood.

Loren's eyes bug. "You caught him? Gave him some hurt?"

"I caught him, but this is my blood." He pulls a jagged wooden splinter from his palm. He wraps his shirt around his hand. "Most of it."

"What is going on?" Tom looks to Mitch, who takes a big pull on a fifth of Jim Beam.

"Alvin's helped us do a little job here. Scaring the shit out of some Basque squatters."

Alvin knots the shirt tight. "There's more to it. I got the whole picture."

"You speak Basque, Alvin?"

"No one speaks that shit. Fella at the rodeo told me a joke once. The Devil himself tried to learn that language and after seven years all he knew was 'yes' and 'no'."

Tom shakes his head. "I don't get it."

"That's the point." He pulls the makeshift bandage tight. "I speak some Spanish and so did Andoni. That was the little jackrabbit's name. *Aye un rancho en Dayton. Se llama El R Perezoso.* The *jefe* is named Tartaro."

"Tartaro?"

"He runs a ranch down in Eldon Corners. The Lazy R. He's the foreman – the boss. Tartaro pays the wages. He drives them to the ranch in his truck. He even charges them to flop here."

Mitch takes another pull. "So, you're saying...."

"He's the one we got to convince. If we want to finish this job. If we want to do it right."

"I don't know," Loren stutters. "I was in for banging on some creeps but...I don't know."

Tom asks, "We going to do this, Mitch?"

"Yeah, Mitch," taunts Alvin. "We going to finish this?"

Mitch swallows, coughs. "Well, yeah...hell yeah! You two follow in Tom's car. We'll pick up the Chrysler later. We're going to kick some ass."

Loren chucks Tom on the back of the head. "You got your guitar, Tom? Maybe you can write a song about it? Ballad of Tartaro!"

Mitch laughs. "Put your guitar away, Burl Ives! He's just shitting you."

Loren apes playing a guitar. "Tom's a regular troubadour, Alvin. Getting pretty groovy on us."

Alvin climbs into his truck. Tom feels like his feet are frozen to the ground. "That kid, he say anything else, Alvin?"

Alvin revs his engine. "Just that Tartaro is going to kill us."

*   *   *   *   *

Tom drives, eyes fixed on the taillights of Alvin's truck as it tears up the highway. Calling to him from the backseat is the guitar, reminding him where he'd rather be, at home, alone in his room, picking out a new melody. Maybe he could set one of his favorite poems to music.

Into the dangerous world I leapt
Helpless, naked, piping loud,
Like a fiend hid in a cloud.

His grandmother calls him "Sunshine." All kinds of people call him that. Teachers, greeters at church. His girlfriend says he is "sunny."

Then why did his heart jump at the words, *like a fiend hid in a cloud?* William Blake! Damn.

"Where did Alvin learn to fight like that?"

Loren pounds a beer with shaking hands. "Probably up at the Castle."

"No shit! Preston, the industrial school for boys? I should have known he'd spent time in juvie hall. That's a hell of a work camp. Nobody could get that tough all on their own. Jesus. He steal a car or something?"

"I hear he stuck a rattler in an old timer's mailbox. The thing bit that geezer right on the lip. They saved the guy, but not the lip. It just fell right off."

"I hear he's being playing backseat bingo with Mitch's stepsister down at The Sagebrush."

"Don't say nothing about that. You know how Mitch is about Madeline."

*   *   *   *   *

43

The radio is playing loud in Alvin's truck. The same corny ballad that's on the radio all the time, the new one from Billy Clover. Guitars and violins swell as a deep voice intones, *"the stage is bare. The lonely crowd wanders home. His jacket is empty and his crown stands alone."*

"Stick to the rockers, Billy." Alvin checks his hair in the mirror. Blacker than black. He doesn't mind when the boys call him 'Elvis.' They're right. He's got the looks. It's his hair that does it. Blacker than black. Darker than dark.

The sweet voices of The Jordanaires swell in harmony, *"Oh, the King is gone. The King is gone, gone, gon—"*

Alvin snaps it off. Silence. White lines flash under the spinning wheels. The boys stare ahead at the road, both lost in their own worlds.

"You and me have never been friends, Mitch."

Morning light begins to creep up the horizon. A single cloud floats among the darkening stars. They're driving in the middle of nowhere, green fields surrounding them. Mitch doesn't take his eyes off the road. "I guess not."

"We're about to get a lot closer. Something like this, it creates a bond."

"Whatever you say, Alvin." Mitch's voice is flat, all the enthusiasm and energy of earlier drained out of him.

"We'll be in good with Mr. Bolles but there's more to it. It's a baptism of fire. And fire bonds."

Mitch's eyes droop. "Yeah. We're going to be chums."

The engine screams. Alvin floors it. Flat out. "Then let's get on with it!" He violently spins the wheel, turning abruptly onto a dirt road. Up ahead is a locked gate flanked by miles and miles of barb-wire fence.

"Shit!" Tom pounds on the brakes as they skid past the sudden turn-off. Loren bounces off the dashboard.

"Where'd they go?!"

The sedan jerks backwards down the highway. Tom steers onto the bumpy road. His headlights illuminate a busted gate; one half torn right off, the other mangled and swinging wildly. The truck is parked sideways in a field, dust settling around it.

Alvin appears in their beam. He makes the 'kill it' gesture across his throat. Tom dutifully kills the engine.

The truck's side door swings open. The window is shattered and there's blood on Mitch's hair and face.

"Mitch?!" Tom shouts.

"Aw, he just bumped his head." Alvin pops the top on a beer and takes a long drink, shaking his dazed head. He tosses one to Mitch who grabs feebly, missing by a mile.

"Hear that, boys?" Alvin cups a hand to his ear. "That's the sound of the dumbest beasts on God's green earth."

The boys become aware of a low mewing. As their eyes adjust to the darkness, little white blobs materialize in the fields around them. Hundreds of milling sheep.

"Sheep, boys. They don't recognize danger when they see it. They have no idea that we've come to fuck up their world."

Mitch leans over and wretches. His pants and shoes are covered with vomit. "Oh," he chokes out, "mama."

Alvin raises an eyebrow, and the other boys laugh. The laugh is hard and mean, fueled by anxiety and anger, a just expression of the incredulity of their situation.

The lonely cloud explodes, letting loose a torrent of rain.

Alvin turns his face toward the falling rain. "Grab some ropes out of the back of my truck and let's have some fun."

The boys pull coiled ropes from the truck. Immediately drenched, Alvin chooses a heavy chain.

Howling like wolves, the boys run wild, beer spilling from their hands, swinging ropes in the dark. Charging the sheep. The weighted rope-ends snap. The rest drags in the mud behind them.

The sheep run blindly, mewing, headed for the only escape, the gate. The shattered gate.

"Get them sons of bitches!"

Slipping and sliding in the mud, the boys follow the panicked animals. Their laughter edges on hysteria. They attack the bottleneck at the gate. Crazed with fear, the sheep climb over one another, pushing through the gate and onto the freedom of the highway.

A lone car crests a hill and swerves wildly. No luck – he clips one of the sheep, spinning its white form in a crazy dance, head chasing tail in a bloody whirl.

Just like a switch being thrown, the morning rush begins, and the road is suddenly alive with cars and trucks. Sheep scatter and fly. Windshields crack. Blood-soaked carcasses are caught in the wheel-wells of ten-ton trucks and emerge twisted and torn apart.

A ewe with crushed front legs and a broken neck kicks her body, head-first, across the slick red asphalt. Headlight beams briefly light the hellish scene before abruptly casting their beams heavenwards as wheels bounce over struggling masses.

The sadistic synchronicity that produced this traffic convergence slips, and the road is empty and dark for miles. The sound of revving engines and squealing brakes subside and there remains only the pitiful screams of the dying.

Mitch lets loose a pleading wail. "Stop! Stop!"

Alvin stands alone in the field, his back turned to the carnage on the highway, watching and waiting. He speaks to himself, barely above a whisper. "Tartaro...I presume...I want to thank you... thank you, you say...why yes, I thank you..."

His voice dips into a mumble, words dripping from his lips, as a battered grey 4 x 4 bounces across the field towards him. "...opportunity... proven abilities...one bad ass... what must be done..."

The rain climaxes with one last heavy burst. The retreating cloud reveals a glowing scarlet sky in the pre-dawn light. A dozen ranch hands pack the rear of the bouncing truck, some hanging from the cab. The windshield is cracked and caked with dirt.

A huge man steps from behind the wheel. Even backlit by the growing sun, his features are clear. A western shirt with pearl buttons. A belt buckle with a giant turquoise stone. A long knife in a sheath on his belt. Silver rings on his meaty hands. Scars.

"What the hell are you doing here? Where are my sheep? You scare them off?"

"Thank you."

"What you saying?"

"I want to thank you, you lousy bastard. You make this all worthwhile. If this thing had been easy – what would that prove to anyone."

"*Basco!* You crazy, boy!"

A car shoots past. For the first time, Tartaro sees the splattered sheep on the highway. "*Chingada!*" Tartaro shouts orders and his ranch hands rush for the road.

"You're starting to get it now, aren't you, Tartaro? You and me are going to have to go at it. And I hope you cut me at least once with that big knife. I'd like a scar to help me remember this night."

The big man steps towards Alvin. The other mud-covered boys keep a good distance between the combatants.

Tartaro stares. "What you want?"

"I want your men the hell out of Washoe county. That way my

guy is happy, my boys here are happy, and only ones dead are a couple of stupid shee—"

Tartaro tosses a fast jab. It catches Alvin square on his nose. He stumbles backwards and lands on his ass. He leaps up, but Tartaro pulls his shirt over his head and twists. The big man's boots connect with Alvin's ribs. Bones crackle.

Alvin falls to a sitting position. Tartaro twists the shirt tighter and delivers two savage knee jabs into his draped head. Swinging his big knife, Tartaro sends the blade glancing off Alvin's kneecap and into his thigh. Alvin howls in pain, gripping his leg.

"This is your boss, huh boys? He looks like Elvis. Elvis is dead, Cabron. This one, he bleeds just like a pussy."

Tom stares in horror as Alvin rolls on his back, Tartaro's boot pressing against his neck. Alvin can't breathe. He closes his eyes. A vision appears through the gathering haze.

It's Mika, dancing above the river, toasting Alvin with his beer. Alvin spits blood, chuckles, "that rascal..."

A chain appears from behind Alvin's back, swinging in a wide half-circle, headed right for Tartaro's face — it wraps around his neck, it smacks him in the teeth. The big man struggles and staggers back, slamming into the open tailgate of the Studebaker. Alvin rides the chain up to a standing position.

Alvin charges and the two men fall into the truck. Now the ends of the chain are wrapped around both of Alvin's hands. The light truck rocks as they struggle.

Tartaro spits between bloody teeth and grasps at the chain. It digs deeper into his neck. He scans the field for his ranch hands, but they are distant dots on the highway, chasing the remaining sheep. His eyes roll. Alvin puts all his weight against the chain.

"The son of a bitch is stonewalling me! Kick him in the balls!"

Loren delivers a powerful punt kick into the struggling man's testicles. Tartaro grunts. A wet spot appears on his pants.

"Another! The bastard ain't home yet!"

Loren punches Tartaro in the crotch, one, two, three times. Warming up to it, he follows with one to the gut and then to both sides of the ribs. Urine soaks the big Mexican's tight jeans.

"That's enough!" Tom grabs Loren and pulls him back. Tartaro flails and kicks Tom in the chest. Tom's eyes flash with sudden anger and the young linebacker throws his weight at the gasping man like he was a practice sled. Something snaps.

Tom steps back, eyes wide in horror. He feels like he's dreaming. Or maybe he's remembering a dream. Someone is missing. A boy is missing. Tom could almost see him disappearing. Not the boy, just the empty space. The space where he was before he disappeared. The dream was lush and green but the shape was grey and fuzzy. The boy-shaped void.

Like a fiend in a cloud...

Alvin leans close to Tartaro's face. He drops the chain and the limp body. They hit the truck bed. A loud clank.

"Holy shit, Alvin." Mitch hacks blood through loose teeth. "Holy shit."

Alvin slides down the side of the truck. Triumphant but spent. "Son of a bitch took a leak on my jeans."

"What just happened? What the hell just happened?!"

"Like I said, Mitch. Just finishing things."

"Aw Jesus, Alvin. There is no big shot, there is no job! Bolles doesn't know shit about this. This was all a goof, a fucking joke, man!"

Alvin feels a big block of ice on the back of his neck. It's melting and trickling down his spine. The ice water is freezing cold and he knows where it's headed – towards the only warm place he knows, the warm place inside him.

Loren shouts at Mitch. "You fucking liar! Why did you do this?"

"He screwed Madeline. He screws them all."

Tartaro's body falls from the back of the truck, landing in a huddle. Tom's voice sounds strange. "He's dead? Really dead?"

"He's dead!" Mitch lifts Tartaro's lifeless head. It is covered with blood and the eyes stare at nothing. "The guy shit and pissed himself, he's dead. Alvin fucking strangled this son of a bitch, and you two socked him good!"

Alvin sucks air though bloody nostrils. "You're right. They socked him good. I killed him. And you stood there pulling donuts out of your ass."

"You fucking idiot. Did you really think they'd go out and build a casino now that you've paved the way for it? Are you that fucking stupid? We're all going to be dead and buried and those fucking cabins will still be there, full of stinking sheepherders."

Loren speaks up. "It's on you, Alvin."

Alvin feels the ice settling in his belly. "How you figure that?"

Loren's voice is steady and calm. "That's just the way it will come down. We can stand here and make all kinds of plans and promises, just the four of us, but if they pin this on us then other people will get involved. Our daddies will start talking to us. Lawyers. You know it'll end up being all about you. You planned it. You killed him."

Mitch agrees. "Sure. Broken home. Prison record. All of it."

Tom's hands shake uncontrollably. He stares at them as the convulsions spreads up his arms, into his shoulders, his neck, his jaw, teeth chattering, he pushes out the words, "You got to leave town, Alvin."

Mitch nods with a sick grin. "Nobody's gonna miss you, except maybe those scags who let you play Don Juan with 'em, who buy your whole bullshit lone wolf routine, pretending you're some great lover down at the drive-in. Well, that's over. That greaser look died with Elvis. You're king of the losers in Nevada and that's over too. You gotta run, boy."

Body shaking, Tom wonders if it will ever stop. What is this feeling? He grabs it. Terror. A whisper now, "you gotta go, Alvin."

Alvin feels the ice take form. A sharp mirror in which he can see things clearly. It's finished. Everything before this moment is gone. Tom is right. Mitch is right. He's going to have to leave town, leave everything he knows behind. And right now. This very morning.

But somehow the warmth is still there. The ice will melt. He was right. He knew it all along. He is special.

He takes a deep inhale and lets it out with a bloody bubble from his cracked nose. "Well fellas, I guess things didn't go our way." He takes Tartaro's knife and offers it to Mitch. "A souvenir of our little adventure."

Mitch reaches but Alvin, quick as a rattler, nicks his face with the blade. Mitch touches his check, a small cut, but deep.

Alvin puts up the gate on his truck and, leaning heavily against it, he latches it shut. "You will be seeing me again. You better just hope I'm not limping when you do." He pulls himself behind the wheel. "The big guy was right. Elvis is dead. Stay away from the bad eggs."

He starts the truck. Wheels spin, spitting dirt. He jerks the wheel and steers the truck in a tight donut, spraying dust all over the boys.

Alvin pulls onto the road and pauses at the highway. The ranch hands are still scrambling to round up the sheep. Alvin guns the engine, heading south, away from the distant glare of Reno's sprawl.

Well past the hands and down the road, he toots his horn.

Just for Variety

By ARMY ARCHERD

GOOD MORNING: 20th Century toppers foreseeing a big opening week for "Cleopatra"...the Liz Taylor epic is sure to be a chart-buster in an anticipated release at the end of the year...Billy Clover is blowing up...after his top-rated TV performance on Jack Parr's Tonight Show, Billy is hot, hot, hot...his disc "Along Came Billy!" is tearing up the charts...Paramount isn't wasting any time putting the new singing sensation to work in his rumored three picture deal...Billy shares a strong resemblance to the late Elvis Presley...the scarlet-locked Clover will put his golden voice to the test with "The Living Dream"...filming begins next month on the Paramount lot... "Billy brings rock and roll back home on the range," says his manager, 'Big' Sam Thompkins...the teens and the teens-at-heart can hardly wait to taste his country fried rock...sultry Gena Rowlands to star in "The Spiral Road" along with hunky Rock Hudson for UI... producer Jerry Needler explained, "sparks will fly between the two. Remember, Rock is single!"...we shall have to wait and see...

Chapter 3

Always On My Mind

The old man clutches the crucifix so hard that his pale hands turn red, in stark contrast to the faint blue of the rest of his body. So far, he's called it a "key" and a "golden ticket."

He draws a raspy breath and continues. "I heard your music, boy, on the TV show. Whooping and yelling and carrying on. It ain't no good, boy. You are dancing at the gates of hell, the gates of...."

His voice trails off to a whisper.

Billy leans over the bed, placing his ear near his father's mouth. He'd done this before, maybe 10 minutes earlier, and this time the same thing happens. The old man's voice suddenly swells, reaching a near deafening roar.

"Cast out your sins! Come back to God!"

It's a theatrical device. His dad probably picked up the trick from some preacher on his Sunday pulpit along with his rap. But it hurts Billy's ears and it makes him sick. The walls of the tiny room move closer. They are sparsely adorned with three small portraits, all of Jesus Christ, savior of old men and their wayward sinner sons.

The place is a shack, basically. A one room structure among the weeds behind a trailer park chapel.

"Dad," Billy stutters. "Look. I'm real glad you found this...."

"Found *Him!* I found *Him,* Billy. And *He* is always with me, always near."

"It's just that this is so new." Billy doesn't know for sure since he hadn't seen his dad in years, but the best he can tell, this redemption is just over a week old.

"It's all new, boy! I'm new! As new as a fresh born baby." The old man shifts to his new-found preacher voice. "Do you see that now? Do you see the power of His Word? Do you see me like I am now, like a baby just out of the womb, who got no scars or nothing."

Billy doesn't see anything like that. He sees the broken veins on the rummy ruins of a face. He sees the shrunken body and bloated stomach – liver failing before his eyes. He does not see blissful peace in those bloodshot eyes. Only the usual cunning. And the deep mean streak that still at the core of his being.

Billy feels a surge of anger and he's just about to stop pretending and tell his dad the truth. To describe the utter lack of signs of a holy bath of redemption. To show Dad the hypocrisy of hating his music, like a bird kicking a hatchling out of the nest and squawking when he learns how to fly. To remind him of his entire wasted life. To let him have it.

But the old fox erupts in a throat-tearing volley of coughs. Gasping for breath, he raises his body painfully, leaning towards his son, hands reaching out. "The Angel! He is coming for me now, Billy……he can take you up as well! Don't you see him, Billy? He's standing right behind you….he's reaching out his hand…." He collapses back on his pillow.

It is quite a performance. It is his last.

*   *   *   *   *

Now, Billy kneels beside a hospital bed with crisp, freshly washed white sheets. Pretty nurses and a wise chaplain watch at a respectful distance. A single beam of sunlight shines through the window and on to the beatific face of Jason Robards.

All in brilliant technicolor.

"Come closer, son." With a trembling hand, Jason brushes the face of his loving son, the singing sensation and prodigal son, Billy Clover.

In the audience, Billy lowers his eyes. The crowd seated around him grows silent and rapt as he studies the weave of the theater's carpet.

Why did he tell Sam about this business with his dad? Why did he agree to do this scene? He looks up, only to see a big close up of his own face, his eyes filled with tears.

A gasp and a squeeze from the girl beside him. This is Mona, a pretty brunette, his co-star and date for the Hollywood premiere of *The Living Dream*.

"Play that song for me, will you?" Jason Robards stifles a cough with a brave smile. "You know the one." He slowly sinks back into the bed, his eyes growing dim.

"I don't have my guitar, Papa. Hang on, Papa, I don't have my guitar...." The packed house catches its breath as one. Big Sam flashes him a big smile and a thumbs up. This is a role written for Elvis. Everyone wanted the script, but Big Sam got it.

"Wait, Papa, wait..."

"I'm sorry, son. Your father has gone to his reward."

Billy presses his face into the sheets, his perfectly coiffed ginger hair moving gently as he sobs, and a choir sings softly somewhere far away.

A slow dissolve to another scene. A beautiful fall day in a picturesque cemetery. The yellow-brown leaves seem to glow in the morning sun.

Billy, looking sharp in a long black coat, gazes at the horizon. Mona, in a white petticoat skirt and blouse, rushes into his arms.

"The Craggy Hills Gang is all rounded up. After you beat Jimmy Graham in that showdown, the rest just gave up."

"What about the bee-boppers? Do they get their malt shop back?"

"Old man Johnson opened it up this morning! Sodas on the house!"

Billy wipes a tear from her eye and places his hand against the coffin.

"This one's for you, Papa."

As the coffin slowly descends into the open grave, and the mourners quietly weep, Billy picks up a guitar and begins to play.

"There's a cabin by the lake, no sight is ever prettier, than the view from her win-der, with lovely Susie by my side, and a pinto pony hitched out back, out back of a cabin by the lake. Just like Papa told me, told me about a cabin by the lake."

* * * * *

"And here he is! The newest star in Hollywood! I give you...Billy Clover!" Big Sam is on top of the world. He leads the applause from atop a table as a band in brightly colored jackets launch into an upbeat "Cabin By The Lake."

The sharply dressed crowd climbs to their feet as Billy enters the famous Musso and Frank's. The restaurant is a place of legends. Bogart, Sinatra, Faulkner, Lizabeth Scott, Chandler were regulars. Billy sure looks like Hollywood royalty in his tight-cut silver dinner jacket and black silk shirt, black jeans, black boots. The main room has been cordoned off for "The Living Dream" after-party. Hay bales replace tables and chairs. Rotating lights project constellations on the walls. Two plaster ponies flank the band who now segue into "Big River Rocking." A cardboard placard hangs below the mane of another horse situated near the service door reading "Hammer," Billy's trusty steed.

The cadre of photographers blast Billy with a barrage of popping flashbulbs. He blinks, momentarily blinded.

"Take my hand," says Mona in a low, comforting voice as she leads him through the forest of grasping execs and supporting players. 'Rumored to be dating', Mona is, in fact, more like a big sister. Her father is an accountant to the stars so Mona grew up in Bel-Air with the likes of Gary Cooper and Cary Grant sitting at her breakfast nook discussing tax shelters and such over coffee and fruitcake. Nothing fazes her.

"Esther Williams on your left. Big smile. She's got the ear of all the gossip gals."

"Esther! You look beautiful. Want to take a cowboy to the rodeo?"

Blowsy and over-dressed, the aging star gives Billy a smooch on the cheek and grabs his ass. The music and the crackle of her crinoline dress drowns out the rest of her come-on. Mona pulls him away.

"Eddie Fisher," she whispers. "Quick handshake and move on. He's mooning over his break-up with Liz Taylor. The man is a bore when he's drinking."

"Great flick, lover boy! Jus' great..."

"Hang in there, Eddie." Billy side-steps a bear hug and crashes right into Vic Morrow.

"I got ya, Billy," Vic roars, his grey whiskers wet with whiskey sodas. "'Someone put a nickel in the jukebox. I want to see if this cowboy can dance.'" It's a line from the film as Pop (Vic) fires up the soda pop gang.

Billy freezes, grasping for an appropriate bit of dialogue to respond with. All he can come up with is a lame "cabin by the lake..."

Big Sam is shouting about the band winning a contest of some sort. Grand prize – playing for Billy at his big premiere. The band members don't look elated as they play some cover or another. "Make room for the man of the hour!" The crowd steps back, leaving Billy in the center of the room. Mona lets go of his hand, applauding as she joins the cheering moviegoers.

Billy makes a cursory bow. The applause grows. They want

more. He spins on his heels. It feels good. He spins again, hands out at his side. 'Everything's new!' repeats in his mind. Like lightning crashing down on all sides, licking his boots, keeping him dancing. "Everything's new!" transforming into an elated shout before settling into a calming mantra. The phrase rushing through him, over and over, bearing acceptance and joy.

He spins once more, into a crouch – something he learned from an old bronco buster. The crowd goes wild.

Billy's life has been a non-stop volley of "new" since he jumped that train, saying goodbye to home and family. A fast rise in Western Swing, a faster decline, playing anywhere and any angle for few bucks, extras in cowboy westerns, and now the Star.

Nothing has really changed. He does what he always does. Takes the ride. Sees where it lands.

"Let's find out who the lucky gal is!" Big Sam spins a barrel full of tickets. A sign reads "Win a Kiss with Billy! He lifts out a heaping handful. "And the winner is...ALL OF THEM!"

On cue, the door crashes open to the street and three dozen screaming teenage girls descend upon Billy. It's a bit. They are all paid. Fake. But the fear Billy feels is real. He dashes into the kitchen. The manic mass of girls follow, caught up in the act. Cooks dash, dishes crashing everywhere.

Billy is ahead of them. He pushes an off-color tile on the wall between the freezers. A panel parts, swings open – a secret door left over from bootlegging days.

Billy's bootsteps echo in the sudden silence of the low-ceiling hallway. Long strides slow as he catches his breath. Warmth washes over his body as he opens the door at the end of the hall and enters a familiar room.

Small, windowless, cigarette burns on the carpet. The only furniture a piano and some scattered folding chairs. A spittoon and a pile of empty bottles. Billy hasn't been here since 1951, but it feels like home.

He's not alone. The members of the party band slouch, smoking, hardly looking up. Their mis-matched outfits let Billy know that they are assembled from a bunch of different bands. Their unimpressed looks tell him that the "winning band contest" was bunk, just like the gals in the kissing contest. A particularly snide-looking saxophonist, baby fat jowls and fuzz aspiring to be a goatee, fast fingers some bebop scat – message sent: 'I'm hip and you're not, Tinsel Rocker.'

Billy can only smile. His street jazz cred is impeccable. "You know where you're standing, Sonny?"

The kid with the sax blows some smoke in Billy's direction. "It's a room," he says, flatly.

"Yeah, a room." Billy's voice is loud but calm. "A room where Bud Powell killed it on that piano, sometimes sharing the keys with Duke Jordan. Kenny Clarke is beating out a kicking rhythm on that chair there. Lester Young blowing with his back against the wall. Dexter, Max Roach, Miles. All just jamming after their gigs when the clubs and the bars are all closed. And sitting right there, with his trumpet, is Dizzy Gillespie."

Billy points to a chair at the back wall. The kid sitting in it stares at his own trumpet. Unlike the others, the kid isn't feigning boredom. He's buzzing with excitement. Sitting down across from him, Billy can see he's much younger than the rest. An ever-closer look and he can see that he is a she. Barely a teen and hiding her long hair up under a pork pie hat, she has bright blue eyes that sparkle with delight at the specters jamming after midnight. "So..." she whispers, "a sacred place."

"That's about right." Billy moves his chair closer. "Mind if I borrow your guitar for a minute, pal?"

The string-bean guitarist hands him an electric guitar. Billy pulls out the cord to the amplifier and plucks the strings hard and loud. After a quick exercise up and down the fret, he settles into a simple, sturdy rhythm. "Follow along with this."

The trumpeter matches him note for note with slender but strong fingers.

"Now close your eyes," Billy says soothingly. "It's okay, just close them and keep playing." She does. "This is something Billy Wendell taught me in this very room. You wouldn't know his name. A family man – five kids – he worked at the auto plant in Downey, but he couldn't resist a late night here with the gang. He probably taught half the guys in the room, and he was kind enough to pass along his wisdom to a kid who lucked his way into the holy after-party, back when I was just about as green as you. Now, it's my turn."

"But..."

"Eyes closed. Play this simple progression. Play it as long as you want. We got all night." The girl's head slowly nods in time, a dreamy look on her face. "Listen to what you hear, what you're hearing inside, and when you feel it, just let loose. Follow the tune you hear...."

She plays. Something simple but with some wild tangents.

The boys in the band slowly join in. All of a sudden, the room is full of the joyous sound of creation.

Billy slips out the back. His work is done.

*   *   *   *   *

High in the Hollywood Hills, Billy leans into the floor-to-ceiling window, more than a little drunk, his face pressed against the glass, staring out into the dark night. The view stretches out from Sunset Boulevard all the way to the horizon. Billy dips a finger in his drink and draws a wet line of 12-year-old scotch on the pane, tracing

Western Avenue all the way through Hollywood, past Wilshire, through sleepy residential houses blinking off, only streetlights there, further down to Pico, Olympic, the all-night drugstores, and finally the ever-burning fire of red yellow and bright white – the Western Strip.

Billy checks his watch. Two AM. The Oasis is closing soon, the band playing a last number, something soft and tender to send you off into the quiet night. Or screaming loud, pumping energy, daring the dying light to quench their fire, affirming that there is more to this evening. Surely an all-night jam session is in the works.

Maybe one, maybe two, maybe a dozen. In the not-so secret after-hours clubs, the back room of a record store, or a tiny space in the labyrinth of halls in Musso and Frank's. Billy knew them all.

Could he make it? He has a car parked out front and he's got the energy; he's got that in spades. His pulse is beating out a heavy rhythm. But he knows he's spent, wiped out from the spotlight and the crowds, Big Sam hollering and pounding his back, the ever-helpful Mona at his side.

Billy turns his back on the panorama of lights. The sparse room is illuminated only by their light. A sliver desk and matching chair, a free-standing statute of undecipherable design – all modern and expensive – and a severe-looking divan where the pretty Mona is lost in drunken dreaming. Composed even in this state. Billy spreads his jacket over her and gently tucks it against her neck.

Filling his drink from a celebratory bottle from his agent – this is his guest house – Billy slides his guitar strap over his shoulders and returns to the window.

His reflection in the window, superimposed over the city lights, could be an album cover. He throw on a winning smile and toasts his ghostly image. He noodles on the guitar, as he does when he's got energy he can't control. Things change but this remains the same. The guitar is battered by wear but is beautiful. The wood still glows, the strings are tight. His first purchase after his long gig in Stan Kenton's orchestra at the Rendezvous Ballroom in Balboa. He's never parted with it, feast or famine.

Maybe he should write an ode to his guitar. Not too sappy, not too bright. Right down the middle. He slides the glass of scotch down the fret, an impromptu steel guitar move. He's ready.

Picking out notes with his fingertips, he noodles away. Sometimes a tune comes. Sometimes a snatch of melody, maybe some lyrics. In a dreamy state, eyes half closed, he waits.

Nothing.

He concentrates – sees an image in his mind of the people from tonight — a mosaic of faces, all turned towards him. His fingers find a melody and he strums it out louder and louder.

Damn! It's 'Twisting Twins.' His hit.

He grits his teeth, his hand leaping from the strings, slapping out a rhythm on the hollow base, and back to the strings again. Another melody emerges.

'Cabin by the Lake.' Shit!

In frustration, he grabs a pile of sheet music off the desk. Songs his agent wants him to perform. He flips through.

Crap. Crap.

Something by Leiber and Stoller! He scans the notes, humming the tune. No disrespect for these great songwriters but this thing is just half-baked Elvis.

This one looks promising but no, he recognizes it as something Johnny Kidd and The Pirates had a small hit with. Clearly another wannabe Presley song – 'Shaking All Over.' "Just not below the waist," Billy sneers, tossing the stack on the floor.

He takes a deep breath and a long pull on his scotch and tries again. Gently strumming. He imagines deep water, clear and warm. A dark fog envelopes him. As he plays, the water grows murky, dark, diseased. He knows that smell.

It's the dirty pond behind the little shed in the woods back home. His laboratory for creating objects from abandoned liquor bottles. He shakes his head furiously, but the images persist. Now, a lake, far as he can see, black as mud, squawking loons on a vicious wind, water lapping against the house on the shore. Now it's water in the basement, up to his knees, there's blood in the water, the water, the water is blood red—

Billy leans against the desk. His breathing is heavy. His heart pounds. Eyes focus on the last page of sheet music, and he lifts it with shaking hands. He'll play anything. Anything to push away the water – the smell of decomposition. Chord after chord. Speeding through the opening verses to the chorus. He sings, "you're a devil in disguise."

He locks eyes with the image in the window.

"Oh yes you are."

Chapter 4

Return To Sender

The sign hanging on the phone booth in the corner of the pool hall reads "Out of Order." Despite this warning, the phone works just fine.

"You there, Sport? You hearing me all right?"

Sport leans against the back of the booth, the receiver nestled between his shoulder and neck. Blonde hair sweeps casually across his forehead. His white polo shirt and slacks make his dark tan seem even darker. He lights a Lucky Strike and blows smoke.

"Sure thing, boss. You tell Monroe to sharpen his pencil and write this down: The Clam Camp, Oxnard, California, one clam and Swiss omelet, three slices of tomato, side of cottage cheese and a grapefruit. Total: a buck twenty. Next up is Rose's Diner in Ventura…"

Marcus Rydell's gruff voice cuts him off. "Ah fuck that. I'm not taking down your expenses. You square that crap up with Monroe when you do your returns."

"Sure, Mr. Rydell, you pay the chump so whatever you say. The pinball machines and the rubber machines here feel a little light to me. I'll tell you, they got paw marks on the take boxes and magnet scratches on the glass. Not to mention, I found two plug nickels and a couple of quarters with fishing line on them."

"Sport, Dick Tracy you ain't. Just get your returns done and get back here. I need you to take a load of smokes up to Hollywood on your way home."

"Whatever you say, boss. It's your bread." He hangs up. "And fuck…you…!"

Since the tavern is right on the dock, Sport has a view of some battered fishing boats as he takes a seat at the bar. His lips curl in disgust as he studies the old bartender. He's hugely fat, with pitted cheeks and a gin blossom nose. He wears a fisherman's cap. Sport is starting to think the place has a nautical theme.

Sport checks the napkin. Sure enough, the logo reads "Captain Howard's, the best 'catch' in San Pedro."

"Hey good lookin', whatcha got cookin'?"

"Huh?" The bartender fiddles with a hearing aid hidden in the rolls of skin behind one bulbous ear. "Get you something to eat? Rydell's fellas usually get their lunch here."

"Why not, Popeye? Gimme a mayonnaise and onion sandwich on white with a side of egg salad."

A galley style saloon door opens behind the bar, and a greasy short order cook carries out some sandwiches. A filthy apron clings to his sunken frame. Blotchy tattoos map his boney arms. He drops the plates on the bar in front of a pair of dock workers. Roast beef on greasy bread.

"Two Sammys."

He looks sick, like he needs a drink, or just had one too many. He skitters back to the kitchen.

"On second thought, scratch that. Just gimme a pack of Chesters."

The bartender looks annoyed. "One pack of Chesterfields. Will you be charging that, sir?"

"Sure, what the hell, make it two packs. By the way, there's queers in the men's room."

"I beg your pardon?"

"Homosexuals are cavorting in the lavatory. That doesn't reflect well on the appeal of an establishment to a lay person, or someone of the female persuasion. Not to mention decent folks."

He tosses a quarter on the bar and walks out. The bartender flicks the coin onto the floor. "Talk about queer."

* * * * *

Sport has the back door framed in his rearview. He takes a glance and returns to his book. He flips pages — diagrams of karate techniques.

The cook steps into the trash strewn alley. He wears a P-coat over his scrawny shoulders, his stooped neck.

Sport checks his hair in the rearview. Gives his mirrored image a wink. Move over, Steve McQueen.

He kills the dome light and slips on his Italian racing gloves. He likes to think that they are his trademark. He opens the car door and steps out, right into the man's path.

"Holy shit! Alvin?!" shouts the cook.

"Loren! Of all the fucking gin joints, my dear! Who'd a thought?"

"Fuck, this here is a surprise, man." Loren wipes his sweaty face. He looks a foot shorter and 50 pounds lighter than that morning in the field in Eldon Corners. "I'm a little caught off guard. What are you doing in Pedro?"

"That's what Señor Jailer said to me in Tijuana last year." Sport laughs. "Just fucking around with you, old boy. Damn, it's been a while."

"Sure has. When did your hair go blond?"

"Like it?" He spins slowly, a model on a runway.

"I guess."

"All good things come from a bottle. You understand that, I betcha."

"Heh heh, good one." He wheezes a cough. "What happened to your Elvis get-up?"

"Aw, I quit that a long time ago. After Eldon Corners."

"Yeah, a long time ago, Alvin."

"I don't go by 'Alvin' anymore. People call me 'Sport.' I'm hooked up with this organization out of Hollywood. They got me picking up returns on pinball and rubber machines, cigarettes, gumballs. Strictly entry level stuff. But you know me. I got my eye on the prize. What the hell, it keeps me busy..." He tosses a few playful jabs at his old friend. Loren cringes. "Enough about me. What you been doing with yourself?"

"Not a lot. I went into the Navy after...uh...Reno there. Got a section eight and ended up here."

"Caught you with a mop handle up your ass, eh?"

"Huh? No. Turns out I'm cluster..." His voice trails off as he remembers something that confuses him.

"Claustrophobic?"

"Yeah, that's it. I had panic attacks in those bunks and berths. Tight quarters, you know. I hit some fellas. The CO didn't like me from the get-go, et cetera and so forth. Next thing I know...." He trails off again.

"You're here in San Pedro."

"Story of my life."

"So, being a good pal and all, you ever hear from the old boys back home?"

"Can't say I have. Not regularly. Don't know about Tom. Mitch is up in Covina I think, near Mt. Baldy. He's working as a barber, got his own pole."

"Mitch? I'd figure a rich kid like him taking over daddy's dealership."

"I dunno about that. I saw him a year ago at a swap meet over in Long Beach. He was buying a barber's chair. I was looking for some license plates. That's how I've been passing my time. My only thing, next to drinking, collecting license plates. Damn near have thirty-eight or so states, getting up there. Still need Hawaii and

Alaska, of course. And Nevada too, if that don't beat all shit, don't it, Alvin?"

"Like I said before, Loren, folks call me 'Sport' now."

"Sorry, sorry. My mind ain't working like it used to. Memory is shot." Loren pulls a half-pint from his pocket and takes a long pull. "You ain't going to hurt me, are you, Alvin?"

"Not too much." He strikes Loren with a straight hand to the throat, then two chops into the ribs. With his right hand, he spins Loren around and delivers two quick jabs to the kidneys with his left. Loren crumples on his weak legs. Sport follows up with a rabbit punch to the neck for good measure.

Holding Loren upright, he roots in the trash and comes up with a soggy box that once held Pabst beer bottles. He slams it over Loren's head. With his gloved hands, he molds the piss-soaked box to Loren's face. It forms like clay around his eyes, his nose, his mouth, choking out his feeble whimpering.

"Easy there, boy. You should have known I'd be coming. You're like a clock with no hands. Just let it come to you. I'm gonna ease you into this whole death thing here. Just take it in and relax."

Loren's body sags. The struggling grows weaker.

"I know, I know. This place smells like somebody gone and took a big ol' leak. But just relax and take it in. You're dying now and there ain't no shame in that. I let you have that last snort so you should be warming up about now. Just let it flow over you. Take in the warm embrace I'm giving you."

Loren's body grows limp.

"That's it, Loren, just let it go. No more of them Sammys. No more of that roast beef. Just let it go."

Friday

EVENING

JANUARY 8, 1965

7:00 **6** THE RIFLEMAN – Western
"The Hero" is stablehand Colby Vane, who finds the townspeople curiously ungrateful after he kills a notorious gunman. Chuck Connors. Robert Culp.
9 SEA HUNT – Adventure
Two fishmen report that they have seen a sea monster. Mike Nelson risks his life to investigate their story. Lloyd Bridges. Ernesto: Christopher Dark.

10 DEATH VALLEY DAYS -- Drama
"The Mystery of Durango" As a young Navy captain, Steve Jackson is confronted by a vigilante mob that has taken over San Francisco. Charles Starrett, June Dayton.

12 NEWS, SPORTS, WEATHER
13 YOGI BEAR – Cartoons

 SPECIAL MOVIE NIGHT

ELVIS' 30th Birthday Celebration!!!

This special memorial begins tonight:

AT EIGHT

Tommy Sands appears in this live American Playhouse performance of **"Blue Hawaii"** playing Chad Gates, a role written for Elvis Presley before his untimely death. Chad gets in all sorts of rockin' mischief as a tour guide in our 50th state, along with the lovely Joan Blackman. Angela Lansbury. Lani Kai.

AT NINE

Billy Clover stars in a THREE film marathon. **"The Living Dream"** kicks it off with Western fun as Billy and his horse Hammer save the malt shop from The Dalton Gang. Then enjoy **"High Hopes"** with Billy facing high-jinks on Wall Street. Finally, thrill to Billy as **"Barrigan"** in this fast-paced police drama with a blotter full of high-spirited songs.

Chapter 5

Are You Lonesome Tonight

Billy perches in the risers of John Marshall High School, Eugene, Oregon, watching the road crew light the stage with bright spotlights of red, white and blue. The drum kit and the amps are all draped in the same patriotic colors, with some stars and some stripes thrown in for good measure. He holds his breath as a dozen men hoist a giant American flag behind the stage. It's 50 feet tall and 100 feet wide and quite dangerous. There's a running joke among the crew, something like "Betsy Ross is going to kill someone." And she nearly did last night in Washington. That slickster, Scoot, slipped in the scaffolding, grabbing the flag as he fell, riding Old Glory all the way down to the hard floor of the Seattle Civic Center Auditorium. The flag got a few rips around the 45th star but Scoot got it worse. Broken pelvis, body cast. He's still back there in the hospital in Seattle.

And that's what's worrying Billy. Scoot isn't here and Billy *needs* Scoot.

The way Billy has things fixed, Scoot usually lugs in some amps, helps hang the flag and other USA trimmings, and then he'd be out the door, off to do his real job.

Which was shaking the town for some local talent for Billy.

Billy doesn't know what his methods are, what magic he uses, but he never fails to show up before showtime with a comely fan eager to meet Billy Clover backstage. A homecoming princess or rodeo queen, a young widow or a neglected housewife. And Billy welcomes the lucky gal into his private dressing room.

And thus begins the pre-show show. The biggest performance of Billy's night happens there, long before the audience starts wandering in. Using all his charisma, charm and a little Country alchemy, he transforms the gym equipment room or building manager's office into the magical secret world of Show Biz. That's what gets Billy charged up. Focusing all his magnetism and appeal into one bright shining beam – a circle of light with Billy smack in the middle. He reaches out his hand and beckons his comely guest to join him in that circle.

Sometimes he gets a kiss, often a lot more. Either way, it is the performance that he loves, that he craves, that he *needs*.

With Scoot gone, Billy is in a fix. A quick mental inventory confirms what he fears – he's already seduced all the suitable gals on the show bus. The backup singers, the band's girlfriends, even perky Miss Peaches Prescott, the country ingenue of the hour.

No, he's in trouble. It's only a couple hours until show time.

As the crew hoists a banner reading RED, WHITE AND COUNTRY, Billy is out the door.

Cruising his silver Coup De Ville down Main Street, Billy casts a nervous glance at the fading afternoon sun, wondering "where does Scoot find them?" He slows the car in front of a beauty salon, but it's full of older women, each sporting a bouffant. The married kind. Maybe this dress shop? Naw, too fancy. The kind of place a gal buys a dress for a funeral or a baptism, not a roll in the hay with a travelling cowboy singer. There's a restaurant with a parking lot out front but then he'd have to eat and he ain't hungry and doesn't have that kind of time.

He's wondered before about Scoot's ability in this field but only in a passing moment of appreciation for the man's skills. This is different. This is urgent. Tonight's show is important.

Mama is going to see him perform for the first time. After five years, she'll be in the audience. In a few hours.

A painful memory swims into his mind. His last time onstage

without his pre-show ritual had been a nightmare. He can see himself standing onstage, bright and shiny in his rhinestone suit, and stiff as a board. Frozen in place, like a wooden Indian holding a red, white and blue guitar.

He pushes the memory away and parks.

The Hotel Mayfair looks nice. It's fancy enough to mean some dress up clothes but not to require a date. And it has a bar. Maybe some lovely beauty from out of town? He could almost picture her – sitting on a bar stool, skirt hitched up, slowly sipping her drink.

Encouraged, Billy clamps on his crisp, snow-white cowboy hat, gives a tug on his lucky curl and struts in.

It takes a moment for his eyes to adjust to the dark room. He makes out a dozen frames at the bar and more than half appear to be female. That's good. Even better is the poster taped to the mirror behind the bar. "Saturday Night Only! Billy Clover and his travelling All American revue. RED, WHITE AND COUNTRY!" And there was Billy dressed to the nines and looking sharp.

"Scotch. Rocks. The good stuff," he says to the bartender. He's well-dressed and friendly, another good sign.

"Sure thing, Mister. You in town for the rodeo?"

In reply, Billy simply nods his head towards the poster over the man's shoulder. The bartender glances around, confused. He shrugs.

"One Ballentine scotch, rocks, coming up."

The folk at the bar are mainly in pairs. He counts three drinking alone – and all of them women! He sips his scotch and studies them.

The one closest to him keeps scanning the door – clearly waiting for someone. He didn't have time to compete with a suitor. She's out.

The blond with the hair done up high is a little too gussied up for his liking – lots of makeup, nail polish and powder – but beneath it was the curves he digs.

The redhead in the coral pink cocktail dress at the end of the bar is a looker, sure, but she has those big eyes, not unattractive, yet Billy has had bad luck with girls with big eyes.

He downs his drink, puts on a winning smile and moves towards the dressy blonde. She gives him a quick glace up through her heavy eyelashes and smiles with a mouthful of yellow teeth, so Billy just keeps walking. He hitches a leg up on a stool next to Big Eyes, resting his hands on his hips, just above his silver-studded belt with the giant gold belt buckle, and smiles. "Howdy, miss."

Big Eyes looks him up and down. "You here for the rodeo?"

Billy nods again at the poster. Jesus, he was wearing the same hat as in the picture!

"You could say I am with the band. In fact, you could say that I *am* the band."

She knits her cherry-colored eyebrows in feigned concentration and studies the poster. "Billy Clover, huh. That you?"

He had misjudged her eyes. They're her best feature. Deep and dark with a speckle of something bright in them. And the rest of her isn't bad either – petite, trim, long legs.

Billy slid happily into the stool next to her, warming to the show.

* * * * *

Tangled sheets, the smell of sex, Billy is wrapped in languid post-coital dreaminess. Nothing can break this feeling. Not even when she asks him for the money.

He isn't surprised. He'd figured it out somewhere in the midst of the lovemaking. Something about the way she moved beneath him, the hint of professional reserve. He was a little surprised to find that he liked that. It added a new flavor to the act.

"First time for everything," he yawns, happily.

"You've really never paid for it?"

"Never had to."

"Why am I the lucky one?"

He stacks some bills atop a pillow. "Don't you worry, ma'am. I'm doing it all for Mama."

"Now, *that's* a first!"

"I mean it. My Mama's coming to the show tonight. I want to rock the house for her." He gently strokes her back. "And, thanks to you, I will."

She tucks the cash away in a red satchel handbag. "How's that work now?"

"I need a charge to get me going onstage. To really tear the place up." He pats her ass. "This here is the best way to do it. The only way."

"You gotta fuck before every show?"

"Only for the last year or so. Used to be the show was what gave me the charge."

"What happened?"

He shrugs. "Something changed." He smiles. "But I ain't complaining."

She gives him a quizzical look then snuggles close. "All you Southern boys talk that smooth talk?"

"Southern?! I'm pure California, baby, born and raised in Sulphur Springs."

"I've never heard of it."

"About eighty miles north of Fresno. Not exactly a metropolis. Mama's flying for the first time."

"Ain't your mama proud enough? Big star like you?"

"Big star? I'm more like a falling star." He motions to a gold medallion around his neck. "Big Sam gave me this. He said he'd add a diamond for every number one hit. I've just got the one." He laughs. "I've been barely skating clear of the 'has-been' label since I was 23, which was two long years ago."

"Naw. I've seen your poster. You're top of the bill."

"Yeah, I'm on top of the heap, and I mean 'heap.' All failed suitors for the King's crown. Yesterday's Next Big Thing – all of them – heartily fitted for Elvis' throne. Good old Tommy Sands, who dyed his blonde hair black and took leg-shaking lessons. He made a movie with Nancy Sinatra, they were going to get hitched, his manager nixed it. Been in the toilet ever since. You don't mess with the Chairman of the Board. Now Eddie Dean, he's a character – Colonel Tom Parker himself dubbed Eddie 'The Golden Cowboy' before anointing him as 'The Hawaiian Cowboy.' Neither really stuck, so poor Eddie takes the stage every night in his metallic yellow suit and a lei, alternating between a jumbo guitar and a ukulele."

"What do they call you?" She tickles his thigh.

Billy swats her behind. "Why, you're looking at a genuine Living Dream. The one and only."

"Are you the next Elvis then?"

"I'm never going to be as big as Elvis. Or as big as Elvis was going to be. But Big Sam and the people who manage me keep pushing for that. And it's just not going to happen. And to tell you the truth, it's exhausting."

"You never know. One big hit, right?"

"Sure. One magic hit, and you're on top. The thing is that everyone around me keeps pretending I'm already there. Already on top."

"You don't like that?"

"Drives me nuts."

"Why not go back to what you used to do?"

Billy laughs. "Walk into a recording session as a back-up guitar player? For a two-day gig? Or play guitar for a week-long gig in honky-tonk bar? People would say, 'is this a joke? Is this Candid Camera?'"

She laughs. Billy hits her with a pillow.

"You can't go back." Billy says, "And this is my big comeback. Haven't you heard?" He stands on the bed, wrapping the sheet around him like the toga of a Roman conqueror. "This British Invasion is going to fail. We'll fight them in the air, we will fight them on the beaches, on the radio and in the concert halls. Big Sam says we cannot lose. Cuz, hell, we all Red, White and Country!"

She laughs so hard it hurts.

"The Beatles play rock n roll with a limey accent. That's why Big Sam decided we need to go full countrified for this tour. Yee-haw!"

"Yee-haw?"

"All this too country for a fancy lady from back east?"

"Back east? I'm from Bakersfield."

"Oh, I've heard of Bakersfield." Billy winks. She fake punches his arm. He fake winces. "We went there for a vacation when I was a kid."

"No one vacations in Bakersfield!"

"Well, we did. My dad set it up. An old house out past Oildale. He sent me and Mama and my brother Donny ahead. Told us he'd be down soon. Never showed up."

"That's strange."

"You want to hear strange? I did some sleepwalking there. First and only time. I somehow ended up in the basement. Something scared me real bad down there and I ran to Mama and woke her up. She loaded us right up and moved us to a motel in town. She told me I probably got scared by the loons at the lake. They made the most awful sounds but I don't know."

She sits straight up. "This house? Down by the lake? Gus Grayson's place?"

"Yeah."

"That's the Murder House! Gus killed like 10 people out there. They called him the Loon Lake Killer. He killed women and children. It was in all the papers when I was a kid. My mom tried to hide it from me, but I knew. Everybody knew about it."

Billy laughs, "I guess that was Dad's plan to get rid of us."

"You really think so?"

"Maybe. But I fooled him. The squawking of those loons was enough. I just kept going from Bakersfield. Jumped a freight train out of there. Straight to LA. Never looked back."

She shivers, pulling the blankets around her. "Now, that's a song for you. Call it 'The Murder House.'"

"I like it." He sings, *"I spent one night in the Murder House! Daddy rang the proprietor, said 'don't let my boy see the dawn'."*

"I was kidding. No one wants to hear a song like that."

"You think so? You'd be wrong. Lots of folks have written country ballads about murder and death and killing. They've been writing them forever."

"You're joshing."

"No, ma'am. I know plenty of them but this is the first one I learned. It's by Jimmie Rodgers." He sings,

"I'm gonna buy me a shotgun
With a great long shiny barrel
I'm gonna buy me a shotgun
With a great long shiny barrel

I'm gonna shoot that rounder
That stole my gal.
Rather drink muddy water
Sleep in a hollow log

Rather drink muddy water
And sleep in a hollow log
Than to be in Atlanta
Treated like a dirty dog."

"Well, you can have it." She pulls tight the straps on her dress. "I'll be going now. Unless you got money for another one?"

"Naw. I'm ready."

*   *   *   *   *

Billy charges across the stage, boots kicking out before him, guitar swinging. He lowers his head, drops to his knees and slides to stop, landing dead center in a perfectly round red spotlight.

The band drops out as one and Billy steps towards the mike. He wipes his face with a handkerchief and shouts, "I love you all!"

The crowd cheers!

"Here's one you may know. We call it "In His Blue Shoes..."

The crowd goes wild! A plump gray-haired woman beams. It's Mama. Billy can hear her voice above the rest. "Billy, oh Billy," sounds so sweet to his ears. Then another voice rises above hers, louder and louder, but not a voice, not a voice at all...

It's the call of the loons.

Chapter 6

A Little Less Conversation

The back of Mitch's house looks like a big, tacky cuckoo clock. Bright yellow with pink trimming and a dazzling red door, which opens and Mitch emerges in a bright Hawaiian shirt, lugging a bag of charcoal.

"Cuckoo," Sport chuckles, peering over the fence from the next-door neighbor's backyard.

Mitch disappears back inside, and the door swings shut, then back open as he reappears with a block of ice.

"Cuckoo."

He drops the ice in a metal tub with the beers and the bottles of orange soda. The door closes. It opens and Mitch wheels out a brass bartender's cart.

"Cuckoo." Sport is cracking himself up but enough of this. "Hey there, neighbor. You wouldn't happen to have an ice-cold lemonade on this scorcher of a Fourth?"

"Alvin! Goddamn!" Mitch suddenly turns a sickly white, clashing with the festive decorations. He gives Sport's attire a once-over – canary yellow turtleneck, blue blazer and sharp jet-black Fedora. "What the hell are you doing here?"

"I'm relocating to the suburbs, my man." He laughs. "I'm just fooling around, guy. I ran into Loren in January, just after New Years, actually. We caught up on old times and he mentioned you were up here cutting earlobes off. Mind you, the skunk said you lived in Covina, not West Covina. Big difference. What the hell, though, took me a while but I found you anyway. You gonna invite me in?"

Mitch hesitates. "Yeah. Sure." He unlatches a gate and Sport strolls on in. He takes a deep breath, breathing in Mitch's life.

"You sure made it outta Reno. Smell that goddamn grass. That is some 'healthy goddamn grass. You have a little shindig in the works? A little *Fiesta* for the Fourth?"

"Just some neighbors. Couple of people from work...some of the wife's friends."

"The wife?"

"Yeah, she's with my boy, Harold. Swim lessons over in Whittier."

"Whittier?! Ain't you got any pools here in Covina, West Covina?"

"Sure. They got pools here."

Sport doesn't answer. Just stares. Mitch unconsciously touches the small scar on his cheek. "Did you want to go inside, Alvin?"

"I thought you'd never ask."

The place is very tidy, except for a few children's toys strewn about. Sport tosses his fedora on the marigold-colored couch and sinks into the plush cushions, propping his freshly-buffed Italian shoes on a coffee table. Mitch hurries over with some beers. "So, Alvin..."

"Please, call me Sport. Everyone does. It's like a moniker that's stuck with me for being a good guy and so on. I rely on my personable character in my line of work."

"And that is...?"

"Collections. Collections and enforcement. I basically go around and make sure certain sordid types stay in line with my boss' investments. Hell, earlier today, I was making a pickup in Santa Anita and you wouldn't believe the shit some of these finks try and pull." Sport admires the shine on his shoes. "It's all about trust in this business. Since I saw old Loren, my boss gives me a little more room to expand my methods. Forgive the smell, but I'm dabbling in Arson. Damn hard to get the smell out of you."

Sports toasts with his beer.

"It ain't hair but it's a living." He lets the dead air hang between them before, "I hear you got your own barber's pole."

"Sure, sure," Mitch says, eager to break the silence. "I have a place in town. Downtown West Cove. It's in a parking lot, but what can I say, that's downtown for you. There's a Sears off Beverly there, so it's nice. Nice and convenient. But we aren't too remote. Good bowling, good school, we're close to the ten. Come see you in Hollywood in twenty minutes."

"Yeah, I'm right there off Franklin and Argyle, right by that new Capitol Records building."

"The round one with a point? Looks like a stack of records?"

"Goddamnit to hell! I done did it again." Sport stands and picks up his flattened hat. "I've sat on this son of a bitch four times since I started wearing it. I think it's finally done for."

"That's why they call it a crushed Fedora, eh?"

"Yeah, sure Mitch. I guess you knew this day's been coming."

"Excuse me?"

"You gone and built this life up for yourself with the career and the kid and the wife and all. But sooner or later, I was going to find you. Wherever you went, I was coming. I would have found you in Reno or LA, off the 99 or the 395. Now, if you had headed to Texas or someplace else, you may have clocked a few more years on me. But I knew you wouldn't get far. 'Go West, young man.' Horace Greeley and all that ring-a-ding."

Mitch fiddles with his bony fingers. Barber's fingers. "What happens now?"

Sport drops his beer and grabs Mitch by his Hawaiian shirt and tosses him through the sliding glass door. Mitch topples with the shattered glass onto the patio.

Sport steps through the empty frame, picks up the stunned man, and throws him back into the house. He pulls a sap from his pocket and sends two swift blows to Mitch's forehead. He goes down.

"Stay down!"

Sport pulls a switchblade from his back pocket. First, he cuts the sofa. Then the recliner. He topples the Hi-Fi. Then the TV. The tube bursts on the carpet. Sliding his knife along the wall, he rips the wallpaper, pulling it off in jagged shards and big strips. The kitchen utensils crash to the floor. A sideways kick breaks the glass in the oven door. He smashes a blender, a toaster. He opens the refrigerator and dumps the contents. A bowl of guacamole splatters over his feet.

"My new shoes! Goddamnit!"

Mitch staggers to his feet. Sports tosses frozen steaks at his head. He pitches the ice cubes trays and frozen vegetables. Mitch weaves down a hallway, clutching the walls for support. Sport grabs a carton of Rum Raisin ice cream and follows. He kicks Mitch in the ass. Mitch falls into the bathroom and Sport tosses the ice cream after him.

"Please..."

Sport leans over, grabbing Mitch by his belt and collar. He heaves the semi-conscious man through a glass shower door. Mitch hits the tile hard.

Mitch blinks, fighting off unconsciousness. There's a large shard of glass protruding from his chest. He blinks again and sees Sport smashing the toilet seat, the mirror.

Sport leaves the room.

Mitch breathes hard, black clouds gathering in the corners of his vision. He hears more smashing and bashing from the other room.

Sport appears in the doorway, wielding a shotgun.

"Found this under the bed." Sport checks the load. "That was a big-league mirror you had in the master bedroom there, pal. Big as a fucking drive-in movie screen. Shit, you could comb your hair all day in that son of a bitch."

Sport levels the gun and blows a hole in Mitch's chest.

Mitch gasps. "Alvin..."

The wheezing sound makes Sport laugh. "Yes...?" He splatters Mitch's face across the white tile.

Sport walks back into the demolished living room. His hat is on the floor, crumpled and ruined.

"Son of a bitch. I can't have nothing nice."

Review of "Still Singing" by Elvis Presley and others

Still Scamming

by R. S. HOWARD

Displaying ridiculously dubious taste, RCA has released this ass backwards collection of odds and ends from the unreleased catalog of Elvis Presley just in time for the 10th anniversary of the singer's tragic death.

I dropped the needle on this disc with the occasion heavy on my mind. And while some songs on this 12 track record, like "Suspicion" and "It Feels So Right," show the promise of what might have been, should Presley have returned alive from Germany to complete them, let me just lay it out, others are complete clap-trap such as a tepid cover of "Fever" and the unremarkable "Soldier Boy."

Filling out the album are covers by contemporary singers whose careers have been modeled after the departed King of Rock and Roll.

RCA's decision to include wannabe Tommy Sands, who sings a passable duet of "Hound Dog" with Eddie Dean, and Billy Clover, hacking his way through a down-beat "Heartbreak Hotel," may prove that the King's legacy lives on, but their inclusion comes off more as an raised middle finger than a tribute.

Crashing RCA's party comes the recent disclosure by Army Private First Class Charles "Chuck" Stockton of the truth behind Corporal Presley's death.

Long been shrouded in suspicion, the death on the munitions' testing site of the Friedberg base, and the Army's insistence that it was an ac-

cident, are brought into question.

The accusations come in the form of a written personal account by Stockton, mailed to the New York Times just days before his death after a long fight with alcoholism.

While the Army furiously denies the allegations of deliberate 'friendly fire', the timing of this final record release is definitely a disappointment for the PR department and jubilation for conspiracy theorists everywhere. To this end, I have to conclude that "Still Singing" is a weak album which, sadly proves that the King is finally dead.

Two stars

Chapter 7

Fools Rush In

Tom knows it's a risk. L.A. is a big city. Big cities have lots of people in them. One of them might be Alvin.

He tells himself that life is full of risks as he watches the palm trees along Wilshire pass his bus window. And it's not like he'd been hiding out all these years. To begin with, he still lived in Reno. Conceivably the first place Alvin would look. He did lie low, avoiding family and old friends, working in a warehouse with only two other fellas, didn't hang out with them after work, didn't hang out with anyone really. Unlisted number, unlisted address.

Naw, he wasn't hiding out.

He laughs at himself as he climbs off the bus. The group stretches, excited – it's been a long ride from Reno. A couple start a chant, "Bobby! Bobby! Bobby!"

The boisterous enthusiasm cheers Tom up. The decision to join these activists and merry makers had been sudden. But he's been building to something like this for a while now. Went to a movie in a crowded mall, drove past the high school. He even took his guitar out from under the bed. He's so out of practice that his fingers don't know where to go.

His fingertips hurt as he struggles to clip a button onto his faded jeans jacket. "Reno is with Bobby in '68!" He follows the rest of his crew into the ballroom of the Ambassador Hotel. A flower-power instrumental version of "Blue Suede Shoes" booms over amplifiers. It is so full of people that he has to focus on the bouncing ponytail of the girl in the vibrant yellow and red kimono if he wants to stay with his crew.

Damn, the place is crowded. He takes a deep breath. "I'll be okay." Safety in numbers.

"Give us a kiss, Captain Midnight."

The bored cop grins as Sport leans against his patrol car. "Hey Sport. Get your greasy mitts off my car."

Sport wipes the car's door with the sleeve of his sharp tan jacket. "Whatever you say, Midnight."

"What's with the 'midnight' shit? I thought I was Officer Gimme."

"That's when you were with Hollenbeck. Officer Gimme More."

"You know I ain't holding bag for Hollenbeck no more." He shifts his Sam Browne belt and farts.

"Naw, you're captain of the Midnight Squad." Sport jerks his thumb at the Ambassador Hotel. It's lit up like Christmas in June. The parking lot is crammed. Judging from the sounds from inside, the hotel is packed as well. The lone patrol car is parked by the entrance. "Where's the infantry?"

"Just me, Sport. Captain Parker is giving this one a pass."

"No shit? Something like this? With a Kennedy?"

"He's still stung over the Gorbachev thing. He took a lot of crap for refusing to shut down Disneyland for the dirty Ruskie. The Captain's not giving anybody another chance to call his boys the 'blue Gestapo.' Let the flatfoots in Detroit and Chicago take that heat."

"You know me. I am not a man to criticize another man's choice. That's how I play it."

"It's amateur night, Sport. Bobby's got his own bodyguards – some Olympic athlete and, get this, Rosey Grier." When Sport shrugs, the big cop continues. "The Rams? Fearsome Foursome?"

"I don't follow the game. Big guy?"

"Huge."

Sport straightens his electric blue silk tie. "Think I could take him?"

The officer laughs. "I wouldn't put anything past you, Sport."

The lobby looks like a puzzle box after some giant picked it up and shook it. All the people are stacked in one corner, far from the star-shaped fountain, near the open bar. Exuberant drunks wave straw hats and annoyed reporters heft heavy cameras by an open door. A crowd is crammed inside the ballroom – these guys aren't getting in.

Sport strolls to the deserted reception desk. He grabs a handful of mints from a bowl and winks at the pert girl in the sharp, candy-colored uniform. "What's the big to-do?"

"Bobby Kennedy just won the California primary. South Dakota too. He's going to give a speech."

"Where's that happening?"

"In the ballroom."

Sport empties the bowl into the breast pocket of a tailored lavender shirt and heads for the elevator.

"It's that way, sir." She points at the crowd. "Through that door."

"Later, gator." He tips his porkpie hat as the elevator door slides shut.

Sport gets off on the second floor. He strolls down the long corridor. He passes a room service tray. A pathetic half-eaten ham sandwich. The door is ajar, twisted sheets on the floor. A western plays on the TV – a handsome cowboy singing in the saddle.

"There's a cabin by the lake..."

Another TV blares from behind a closed door. The news. Not usually Sport's style but, ever since the Tet Offensive back in January, he can't get enough. The somber intonations of the long lists of the dead and injured is a playground for a man of his unique sensitivities and imagination. He can fill in the scenery – jungle ambushes, late night attacks – all colored the bright red of fresh blood.

He opens a door and jogs down a stairwell. Funny that he would finally catch up with Tom here, right in LA! He was the only one who never left Reno. Which is odd. He was the dreamy one of the bunch, with his guitar and his poetry.

Sport has been taking his time with Tom. Let him sweat. Besides, it's a long drive to Reno and Sport is a busy man. Many responsibilities. Mainly, they concern women. Not his favorite thing, but what can you do when you work in a racket like Marcus Rydell's? The women are his bread and butter. The rest of it: the shakedowns, strong arm stuff, torching establishments – that just came with the territory. Just like the jukeboxes and pinball machines. The women, that's the number one asset. So, like it or not, that's how a top guy like Sport spends most of his time.

Sport takes a service hallway to the kitchen. He salutes the cooks and wait staff. "*Hola, amigos.* Just passing though."

Tom would probably still be safely sweating it if Sport hadn't seen the bus. He had just finished up a pound-down on a sloppy pimp at a flea bag hotel downtown and he stopped to clean the muck off his shoes. Snakeskin. Brand new. The bright streamers adorning the bus caught his eye and, of course, the word 'Reno,' his hometown. "Reno for Kennedy."

And who's in the window there, way in the back, probably near the shitter – Tommy boy. The last of the Eldon Corners crew.

Sport guesses it's just his time.

The ballroom is packed wall to wall. Everyone is cheering. Swaying back and forth like waves in a bathtub. A crystal chandelier the size of a VW bug hovers above. Somewhere up front is a stage with Bobby Kennedy and a microphone. His nasal voice bounces around and over the cheers and applause. "Not just a victory in California. A victory for California!"

Sport figures he'll be able to spot Tom and, despite the size and milling frenzy of the crowd, he figures right. Because Tom is so pretty. He always was, even when he was wearing his football jersey, even with the buzz cut all those boys had in high school.

He's even prettier now. At first, Sport thought it was a woman he glimpsed across the room, waving a "Kennedy in 68" sign with his slender, delicate fingers. Sport pushes his way towards him. In his jacket pocket, his hand clutches a knife. He'd planned on getting Tom alone somewhere, having a talk with him like he did with Loren and with Mitch. But that wasn't going to work now. It'd have to be a quick shiv and move on.

He didn't feel too disappointed. To be honest, the joy has sort of drained out of the whole thing. Now, it felt like something he has to do, is happy to get done, but he doesn't anticipate the satisfaction he had experienced with the other two.

There are still a couple dozen people between him and Tom when Sport hears the shot. A light crack. He recognizes the sound – a .22 revolver.

In the momentary shocked hush that follows, he hears a man shouting from the kitchen. "Get the gun, get the gun" and then "hold him, hold him" and "we don't want another Oswald."

Assassination! The spooked crowd goes wide-eyed and wild, surging this way and that. A woman in a smart pink dress is pin-balled in the roiling mass, shouting for help. A campaign worker grabs her arm. "Mrs. Kennedy! Bobby's been shot!" He pulls her towards the kitchen door.

A man bumps Sport hard, exposing his shoulder holster and .38. The man gawks.

Sport thinks, "oh no, don't drag me into this!" and runs for the exit. Mission aborted. Tom will just have to sweat some more.

Moments later, standing in the shadows, his back pressed against the outer wall of the Ambassador, Tom scans the parking lot. He'd only got a quick glimpse of his pursuer before Hell broke loose, but the image is burnt into his eyeballs.

He was a fool to have come to LA. The logical part of his brain had told him LA was a place to avoid. But the logical part was also the scared part, and Tom was tired of being scared. So when Bobby's noble voice on the radio stirred him, he just followed it onto the bus and into the belly of the beast. Now he isn't scared. He's terrified.

As he slips into the crowd following the ambulance into the streets, it is another Kennedy's voice that Tom hears. "We have nothing to fear but fear itself."

Tom has something to fear. Something with a familiar face and a determination to end him. Alvin.

* * * * *

When the U.S. Army Sergeant unlocks the door to the recruiting office, he finds a disheveled man curled up on the concrete. Tom begs.

"I want to sign up. I want to go to Vietnam."

Chapter 8

Green, Green Grass of Home

The burly bartender lines up three shots on the bar. "Welcome home, Billy," he grunts.

Billy lifts the first shot glass, and its contents slide down his throat. The liquor sets off fireworks and his eyes drift towards the trophy mounted above his head. Gnarled antlers threaten malice through a faintly pulsating red fog. Other trophies hang unevenly on the wood paneled walls. A buck, a boar, a ridiculous trout.

Billy raises the second shot. "Here's to the Avalon Tavern, Sulphur Springs, 84 miles northeast of Fresno, California, the site of Billy Clover's homecoming party of one." The bartender has already moved on to another drinker so Billy toasts to the dead animals on the wall and tosses the dark liquor back in one giant gulp.

"Hey Billy, what do you say?" A smiling man leans on the bar. He is a study in contrasts. Coiffed hair and jailhouse tattoos. Short-sleeved plaid shirt and polyester dress pants.

"Dick Dacklyn. How's tricks? Or is it your night off?"

"Hilarious, Billy. I heard you were back in town."

"You heard right." Billy has aged. His hair is full and startlingly red but where his physique was once lean and relaxed, it now reads wiry and wired.

"Something wrong, Billy?"

Billy shakes his head. "No, no. Just clearing my noggin. Hollywood can be a whirlwind."

"I bet. No rest for 'The Living Dream,' eh?"

"You said it, brother. Right now I'm taking it easy, working on some new songs." Billy throws down shot number three and places the empty glass on an untouched notepad. "You still in the pharmacy business, Dick?"

"Well, since you still seem to be in the music business, we may be able to work something out."

"Set me up with a couple dozen bennies?"

"Fifty will cover that. You need any weed?"

"Just the bennies."

"Oh, you dig the uppers. Did you hear about Tommy Sands? He took the pledge after drying out at the Mayo Clinic...."

"Yeah, and his new song blows. 'Clean As Can Be' my ass!"

"No Seconal then?"

"Naw. I'm one of those cats that needs to be up when I'm writing. That's me. I'm on the freeway when it comes to this shit, Dick. No time to slow down once I get started."

"No time to slow down, huh? Even when the bugs start crawlin' out of your skin?"

"Sometimes it makes for a good song."

"What's that one by Porter Wagoner? Not the one about the accident, but the other one."

Billy sings, *"In a building tall with a stone wall around,*
there's a rubber room.

When a man sees things and hears sounds that's not there,
he's headed for the rubber room."

"That's the one. 'The Rubber Room.'"

"Illusions in a twisted mind to save from self-destruction,
it's the rubber room.

Where a man can run into the wall till his strength makes him fall and lie still,
and wait for help in the rubber room."

"Guy sounds like he's got a few screws loose."

"The man can write one hell of a song."

"Didn't you play with Porter?"

"Sure I did. But that was way back on 'Satisfied Mind. 'Skid Row Joe' off the new album, now that's a twisted song."

"Damn, that album cover is something! Gives me shivers. In the Nudie suit, all covered with sweat? That face, man, honest-to-God anguish!"

"You can't fake that. Let's see these English boys top it."

"Shit, Billy, the Beatles are doing fine without your help."

"Their stuff has always been fluff. Now, it's drifted off the planet. Like a little balloon gliding around among the stars. There ain't nowhere to go but down. The music is changing alright, but players like Porter and me know where it's going."

"Going straight to the nut house, you ask me."

"Yeah, when you get good and miserable, sometimes your work will show it. Hell, people love hearing about other people's misery. It sells records."

Dick tosses down a baggy full of blue pills. "Keep popping these bop pills, Billy, and you'll have plenty to sing about."

* * * * *

Maybe a drive will help. Maybe the autumn leaves will ease his troubles. A slow ride on old 299, outside of town. He sticks his head out the window, feeling the air on his stubble, imagining trees waving at him, tossing about their yellow and red leaves in celebration of his return to Sulphur Springs. First time in fifteen years.

He parks on a dusty road by a solitary bridge over a slow-moving river and walks. He kicks rocks. A cool breeze blows through his hair. His breath grows more measured. His shoulder muscles relax.

His mind is clear.

A whiff of stink bug on the air and a memory slips in. Little Billy walking down a country road, could be this one, carrying the carcass of a bike, the wheels gone, stolen outside the drugstore while he was playing pinball. He's headed home to a red-faced, drunken dad with a belt.

Right away, Billy's breath comes in short, shallow gasps.

Maybe coming home was a mistake. He's got enough problems back in Hollywood.

He cashes a bill with the boy at a lonely Gulf gas station. A tourist in a straw-hat pumps gas into a station wagon full of kids. "Excuse me. You Billy Clover?"

"Nice to meet you."

Billy puts out his hand and the guy shakes it. Doesn't ask for an autograph. So that's where he stands these days. No photo with the wife and kids either.

He drops a dime into a payphone a few yards from the pumps. He hunches in the booth, receiver held tight to his ear.

"How's the heat?"

"It's hot, Billy. Rydell is pissed." Walter's voice cracks on the other end of the line. "Lyla ran off with his Continental."

"What's that got to do with me?"

"He thinks you might have something to do with it."

"Lyla has a mind of her own. Besides, how much is the Continental worth? It's a '62 for Christ sake. And it's Burgundy."

"It's Lyla he's thinking about. You know she's always been his favorite. When she's dancing, he's always front and center."

"Well, goddamn."

"Don't sweat it. She'll turn up or he'll calm down. Just give it time."

"I don't have time, Walter. I already spent the advance from Premiere. I got to get them an album quick."

"What would old Sam say?"

"Screw Big Sam. I haven't heard a whisper from him in a year."

Walter coughed up some phlegm. "Word is one of Rydell's goons was asking about you at Gold Star."

"And probably the rest of the damn recording studios in Hollywood!"

"At least the ones you can afford. Which is a small number."

"You're breaking my balls? Now?"

"Sorry, Billy. Just trying to lighten things up."

"I'll have to cut the record up here. I can do it real stripped down. Just me and guitar. Ballads. That shit is selling right now."

"You gonna write ballads?"

"I already got some ideas."

Billy hangs up. He lets out a long breath then treks back to the bridge where he parked the 1962 Burgundy Continental.

He tries to remember last night's dream. He can only grab a few snatches of an unwritten song, *'that night when it all when wrong' something something 'who knew Fate would come along...'*

He shakes his head, drops a rock on the accelerator. The engine screams and tires smoke as Billy leans all his weight on the brake pedal.

In one swift movement, he throws the door open and leaps from the car. It jumps and charges, straight for a fragile wooden railing, through the railing, off the bridge, arcing over the river, then landing, upside-down, in the murky, slow-moving water.

Billy stands on the twisted bridge above, watching the car slowly submerge. He crosses himself and lowers his head. Suddenly, he remembers.

"Aw shit!"

Moments later, Billy emerges from the river, soaking wet and carrying his dripping guitar.

*   *   *   *   *

The convertible Corvair swerves back and forth across the northbound lanes of Interstate 5. The blond, tanned man behind the wheel fiddles with the radio. His blue and yellow plaid scarf flutters in the passing air.

Static. Down Home Gospel Hour. More static. The Beatles.

"Jesus. Even way out here."

The sun breaks through the clouds that have followed him all the way from the Grapevine. Sport slides on some dark shades, tilts his head into the sun's rays. He considers himself in the rearview: here is a man who lives a carefree life.

A country station plays a stirring number. *"The father, the son, and my gal Sally. Old Glory waving on the fourth of July. Mama's stew and Papa's brew. Color me...Red, White and Country!"*

He snaps off the radio. A muffled snort from the passenger seat draws a sneer. The old man has been snoozing away ever since he climbed into the car back at the Unocal.

"Hey old man. Hey granddad!"

The old guy peeks out through half-closed eyes, not yet ready to abandon his nap.

"What can you tell me about these parts, dad?"

"What did you say?"

"All this." Sport sweeps his arm, encompassing the flat land that surrounds them. "What can you tell me about Sulphur Springs? What can you tell me about that hick town, fella? Gimme the local color."

"Where you from?"

"Hollywood."

The geezer nods. That explains it. "Well, Hollywood, I ain't from around here. If I were, I wouldn't need to be hitchin'. I'd have a car or maybe a friend to come and pick me up. I don't know nothing about Sulphur Springs except that's where you said you'd drop me." His eyes flutter, sleep calling. "Any more questions, Hollywood?"

Sport rolls his neck, stretches out his shoulders. "Just one. Pick a number."

"What?'

"A number, pops. Say somethin' between one and fifty."

"Okay. Fifty."

"Good answer." He slows the car, eyes on the speedometer. "Fifty it is."

His hand moves fast. Reaching across the old man's lap. Unlatching the door. Shoving him out. The old man is still half-asleep as he hits the pavement in a roll. The Corvair continues north towards Sulphur Springs, cruising at a comfortable fifty miles per hour.

Chapter 9

Good Rockin' Tonight

A sign reading "Country Lane Studios" hangs outside of a shabby storefront on the once-bustling main street of Sulphur Springs. Better days. The windows are covered with old playbills. Faces peer out from sun-bleached album covers; either freshly shaven fellas in sweaters or freshly shaven fellas in cowboy hats.

> *The caller called Casey at half past four,*
> *he kissed his wife at the station door,*
> *he mounted the cabin with the orders in his hand,*
> *and took his farewell trip to the promis'd land."*

Billy pours sweat on the microphone. He shakes a handful of bennies like a maraca, speeding like a freight train and singing about one that's out of control.

> *He looked at his water and his water was low,*
> *he looked at his watch and his watch was slow,*
> *he turned to his fireman and this is what he said,*
> *'Boy, we're going to reach Frisco, but we'll all be dead.*

Billy pulls off the sweat-wet cans and glares through a pane of glass at the confused face hovering over the recording board. The heavy man sports thick framed glasses and a scruffy goatee. He hits an intercom switch.

"What's the problem, Billy?"

"I can't get into this one. I mean, when did the old number nine crash anyway? Back in 1900-and-something and guys have been singing about it ever since."

Oscar scratches the skin under his toupee. "I guess what you're saying is you don't really feel what you're singing."

"Yeah, exactly. Shit, I got a ton of original material up here." He taps his forehead. "Enough to fill the whole album."

"I understand that, Billy, but we need standards. Something familiar along with the new songs. Besides, that's part of your gift."

"What do you mean?"

"You're a chameleon, Billy, when you want to be. You can hear a guy sing just once, then you can turn around and sing his entire catalogue note for note, just the way he'd do it. It's scary how you do that."

"But it ain't me. It ain't my songs." He leans on the glass. "You don't get it. I've been cold for years now, man. Nothing new coming. And now I got a ton of new stuff. I can't stop it! It's pouring out. And you say I can't record them?!"

"Well, this new stuff of yours is pretty different. It's not like your other hits. Let's face it, it's no 'They Call That Gal My Mama' or 'Twisting Twins' or man, your biggest hit, 'Cabin By The Lake.' Good, wholesome tunes. This new stuff...it's dark, man. It's really dark."

"That's where I'm feeling it, you dig? I gotta follow my muse."

"Well, you've been right before. And, hey, getting dark and edgy worked for Johnny Cash, Porter and the Louvin Brothers. Who knows, maybe it'll work for Billy."

"You gotta trust me. It's 1969, man. Look around. Things are changing. The music is changing. This is where it's headed."

Oscar sighed. "I believe in you, Billy. But you have to meet me halfway. You don't want to take it too far."

Billy nods, sobered. "You're right, you're right." He takes a deep breath. "Okay! Let's cut this thing! Let's shake a tail feather here, Oscar!"

Oscar counts him in. Four, three, two, one.

* * * * *

"I like your old songs, Billy. Have some potatoes."

Billy takes the plate from his mother. She's all dressed- p for dinner in her Sunday dress, even though they are eating in the kitchen. Billy passes the plate, untouched, along to his brother, Donny, in work-worn flannels and heavy boots, just home from work at the mill. The linoleum table is crammed inside the kitchen walls, leaving little room for the three of them.

"I know you do, Mama. But I'm wasting my talents. That Oscar, with his oldies and his songs about God." Billy looks to the heavens. "No offense, Lord. I just don't feel people should be making money off your glory."

"Such a good boy."

Donny snorts.

"It's good to be back, Mama."

"Home sweet Home, Billy."

Billy looks around the tiny house. It's smaller than he remembers. Even the faded pink flowers on the wallpaper seem smaller, closer together. He puts down his fork. "I'm sorry I ain't bought you the big house like I always promised you."

Mama p-shaws. "Oh, stop that. What would I do with a big house? I'd get lost."

He takes her hand. It feels cold. He covers it with both hands. "I'll get you one someday. Biggest house on the block."

Donny chews loudly, snorts again. "Promises, promises. You never got her nothing."

"That's bull, Donny. And what about you? How's that '64 Thunderbird I gave you off the royalties on 'Devil in Disguise?' What about that?"

"That junker? With the cracked tranny and the broken back axle?

100

I parked it in the lot of the 49er Motel years ago. I keep hoping someone will steal it."

"The old 49er, huh? The boys from Cross Creek High still taking their prom dates to that hole?"

Donny blushes. "How the hell should I know?"

Mama pipes up, cheery as ever. "Next time you're singing and playing on one of those TV shows, you should do some of your impressions. You should do Jimmy Hart."

"Mama, no one knows Jimmy Hart unless they grew up on this very block."

"But it's so good, Billy. You sound just like him, and you got his walk down too."

Billy jumps up and waddles back and forth across the kitchen, with wide exaggerated steps. "Hello *tweet* Mrs. Clover," Billy lowers his voice a couple of octaves, whistling between every couple of words, "you know *tweet* where I left my *tweet* pig, ma'am. I'm taking Miss Porker to the *tweet* Sunset Service."

Mama crows and claps her hands. Donny laughs a haughty laugh. "You got lots of hot TV appearances coming up? This your big comeback?"

"Comeback?! Where you think I've been?"

"Your brother was on the 'Hoffman Hayride'. That's Spade Cooley's show. Billy was on that show, twice."

"It's 1969. That show ain't on TV no more, Mama." Donny scoffs. "Ol' Spade's in prison for killing his wife."

"I remember watching you on TV for Christmas. Riding a horse in the Santa Claus Lane parade, right there on Hollywood Boulevard!"

Billy strums his guitar. *"Here comes Santa Claus, here come Santa Claus, right down Santa Claus Lane..."*

Mama grabs Billy's hand in delight. "Gene Autry was riding Champion down the middle of the street and singing that very song. Behind him came all the stars in Hollywood. There's Lawrence Welk, and Mr. Jerry Mathers, and here comes Anne Francis..."

Donny smirks. "Don't forget Dinky the Roller-skatin' Donkey, Mama."

"And there was my boy, Billy. Up in the saddle and looking sharp. Riding with Iron Eyes Cody and that western movie star...?"

"Monty Montana, Mama."

"He was in the *Bat Masterson* episode you done."

"We was in *Gunsmoke*."

"Yes, and then that newscaster come up to you and my sweet boy waved to the camera and said 'Merry Christmas, Mama' for his mother at home. And then here comes Santa Claus, up on his float there. What did Santa say, son?"

"I don't recall."

"He said, 'I love Hollywood people the best!' And he was talking about you. About my little Billy."

Donny pushes his plate away. "Mark my words, Mama. Billy'll be in the poor house by this Christmas. Or the State Penitentiary!"

"What's that, Donny?"

"He's just yapping. You know Donny." Billy leans close to Donny and lowers his voice. "You're right, they'd lock me up in a flash if they knew what I was thinking about doing to you right now."

"Oh yeah? You going to show me?"

"Mama don't know nothing about me. She don't want to hear about the women and my bad ways. Play her game, make her happy, and just let her keep thinking she has something to be proud of. You know as well as I do, I'll never change."

"Elvis never would have gone to hell like you have, getting weird, doing drugs..."

"Don't bring Elvis into this! I've had enough of that."

"What are you saying, son? I can't hear you boys."

"You keep up the way you are, Billy, and you'll break her heart for good soon enough. How you think she'll take it if her oldest boy is found face down in the parking lot of the Avalon Tavern?"

"Beats the shitter. That thing's filthy."

"Keep cracking jokes, Billy. The last joke will be your funeral. The only people there will be me and her."

"What are you boys talking about?"

"Nothing, Mama. I'm just asking Donny to step out to the bar with me. Like lovin' brothers do."

"I'm not going, Mama. I got to sleep."

"You're a lucky man, Donny. You can sleep at night. Not me. I got songs up here." Billy raps his head with his knuckles. "I got to get them out."

"Maybe you should get some professional help, Billy."

"I do." Billy tilts an imagined bottle. "Every night."

* * * * *

Oscar plays the new single in his office. If your prized possessions are a gold record album and a couple of gold-plated bowling trophies, then yellow would be among the worst colors to paint your office walls. Oscar's office is yellow.

The freshly pressed 45 spins on a record player atop Oscar's desk. Billy pounds a beat on his chair, singing along.

"They laughed and they danced at the usual place, neither knowing that she'd soon be sleeping in a watery grave. Oh Lyla, Dear Lyla—"

Oscar lifts the needle. Billy pops a pill and washes it down with a slug from a fifth of whiskey. He looks expectantly at Oscar. "Well?"

"Personally, Billy, I don't get it. I can understand one or two songs about a dead broad. But four? I can't sell that. Maybe at the loony bin, but not in the record store."

"What the hell do you expect from me? A record full of worn-out standards? I told you, that ain't me!"

"Shit Billy, I'd be happy with something with an upbeat tempo. I mean, you decide to do a cover and it's 'Psycho'. Don't get me wrong, I like the novelty of the 'Psycho' single. We might be able to sell that. But it's *all* like that. Out there."

"I gotta go where my songs take me, Oscar. This stuff is coming from deep inside me, dig?" He taps his chest with the bottle, spilling on his shirt. "It's coming out complete and whole and just right. It's like a gift. I thought I had lost my way, but, man, I'm inspired now."

"But why is it so...dark? You're singing about whorin', about shooting up hard drugs, boozing, and this new one, 'Dear Lyla?' That one takes the cake!"

"This track is about lost love and a guy who is ready to die over it. Ever hear of a little ditty called 'Romeo and Juliet'? That one was written by William Shakespeare, mister!"

"When you said you had some stuff going on in that head of yours, I had no idea."

Billy stands, unsteady, rocking on his feet. "You know what, Oscar? You wouldn't have any idea. There ain't too many of us out there that think this way. I wouldn't expect you to see the whole picture." Billy struggles to get on his brown suede jacket. His fingers keep getting twisted up with the fringes on his sleeves. "We shall now part ways. It's been nice working with you, Oscar, and I'm sorry it has come to this. I really am."

Oscar laughs. "Billy, are you serious?"

"Afraid so." He scoops up a stack of singles. "I'll consider this payment in full."

"Clover, you are one nutty fellow. You ever thought about maybe checking into one of those sanitariums? It might do you some good. When you clean up your act, come back here and we'll work something out."

"Oh yeah? Look at Van Gogh. They all thought he was crazy. See you on your way down, Oscar."

The petite receptionist is listening in the hallway, and Billy nearly knocks her over as he careens towards the front door. He pauses to scatter some papers and records across the room. He rips the wooden "open" sign from the window and throws it out on the sidewalk ahead of him.

The room feels very empty after he's gone.

"May I say something, Mr. Lane?"

"Go ahead, Martha."

"That man scares me."

"You and me both."

* * * * *

Billy's going off the rails and he knows it. He's a runaway train with no brakes. "Hold it together, Billy," he mutters.

The drinks are going down quickly at the Avalon. They are just disappearing from Billy's hands. Everything is too bright. Too clear. It's the pills. And the booze ain't helping. But what's he supposed to do? Stop?

He tosses down another. Slams the glass down on the rutted bar top.

Waylon Jennings is on the jukebox. His voice has a sharp crack in it, like cold winter air. He sings about how something is wrong in California.

Dick in his polyester suit sidles up next to him at the bar. "Barkeep, gin and tonic for my friend. A Chivas for moi. And whatever old Billy here is spilling on those native duds of his."

"Dick, you son of a bitch. I've been looking all over for you."

"Billy baby. You know Spike, don't you?"

Billy pops another handful of pills and stares at the skinny hustler. It's so bright inside his head that he sees every detail, every feature in sharp relief. The leather pants and tight shirt, the bright red hair, brighter than his own. The fake mole on his upper lip. The line of stitches above his pencil-thin eyebrows.

"Shit, man, did I do that to you?"

The lovers laugh.

"You idiot, Clover. That was from his last trick."

"Hey, watch your fucking mouth, Dick! I don't even know the guy!"

"That never stopped you."

They grope and giggle. Dick's tongue looms large. Spike's lips pucker and expand, beckoning red and wet.

"Aw hell," Billy sighs. "I'm the Living Dream." His hands shake, spilling his drink all over the place. He gives up and tosses the glass behind the bar. "Hey, Dick. You got what I need?"

Dick slides out a bag full of pills, blue and black and red.

"I need something stronger."

"What you got for me?"

Billy slides the stack of 45s down the bar. "These are singles of my latest. Fresh off the presses. Probably worth a lot. Look. I even signed them."

"I can't give you much for those."

"This one, 'Dear Lyla', is honest-to-God the best thing I ever wrote. Forget 'Cabin By The Lake' and all that crap. This disc is hot, and it will go fast. I already traded one with the bartender for these drinks."

Dick yawns.

"The B-side is 'Psycho'. Blind Leon Payne wrote this sucker. Eddie Novak had a hit with it."

"I don't know. You think Elvis would've done covers? Popped up on speed?"

"C'mon! Check it out!" Billy begins to sing.

"I saw my ex again last night, Mama
She was at the dance at Millers store
She was with that Jacky White, Mama
I killed them both and they're buried
Under Jacob's sycamore
You think I'm psycho don't you, Mama?
Mama pour me a cup
You think I'm psycho don't you, Mama?
You better let 'em lock me up."

The words are slurred but the voice is strong and full of anguish. Dick is moved. "How much bread you got, Billy?"

A wad of bills follows the 45s. Dick smiles.

"That single's sounding pretty fucking good right now, Billy." He shows a row of silver capped teeth. "Shall we take a drive?"

* * * * *

"Cornball," sneers Sport. Cornball place. Cornball jukebox playing cornball tunes. Cornball antlers on the cornball wood paneled walls. A guy like Sport stands out in a cornball joint like this. He shaves for one thing. That one thing alone makes him stand out.

Sport runs his tan hand through his bleached blond hair. He straightens his racing jacket and drops his dark shades on the bar. No one's going to confuse him for a regular, that's for sure.

"Hey guy. Gimme a seven and seven." He pops a toothpick in his mouth, eyes scanning the room. "How's business?"

"Tiring."

"I hear you there. The shit we walk through for a dollar."

The bartender waits for his money. Instead, he gets a view of a black and white glossy of a blonde in sequins and feathers posing on a heart-shaped bed covered with roses.

"Tell me something, Slick. You ever seen this broad around here? Name of Lyla."

"Can't say that I have."

"I believe you. I have a feeling she never made it this far north. That's just me though. My boss wants me to check all the bases, you know."

"No, I don't."

"Sure you do." He laughs. "I have to fly. Maybe I'll see you around. Keep the hose handy after closing, pops."

"What the hell is that supposed to mean?"

"You're a good sport, Harv. I like that."

The needle drops on a record as Sport passes the jukebox. He's got the door open and is halfway out before the lyrics catch up with him.

Some say she done him wrong,
but he never done nothing right.
He told her he loved her and Lyla just laughed.
That's when things went wrong on that terrible, terrible night.

Sport stares through the glass at the spinning 45. 'Billy Clover. Country Lane Records.'

He stole her heart.
He stole a car.
He drove and drove that big Continental
but he didn't get too far.

Two drunks look up as one when Sport laughs. He eyes them. "What do you think of the song, fellas?"

The one closest to the jukebox cups a hand to his ear. "What's that?"

"The song, Grampa. You got an opinion on the song?"

"An opinion? How the hell could I not have an opinion? Some asshole dumped a ton of quarters in there and pushed the same button 30 times."

His drinking pal chimes in. "30 and counting."

"It's about a guy who is wrongfully charged with his girl's death."

"Naw," says his pal. "That's all in the guy's head. He's just expressing how he feels. His girl left him, and he feels guilty. Like he's on trial and sentenced to death."

"Where did you get this idea?"

"Listen to the lyrics."

"I have! For the last hour! You're nuts."

"I'm nuts? You ever heard of a metaphor?!"

They both turn to Sport. "What do you think, mister?"

Sport smiles. "I think Billy's got a hit on his hands."

* * * * *

Things are all tidied up in Oscar's. The bell over the door rings. Oscar stares at the tanned guy in the doorway. The stranger is both chewing gum and sucking on a matchstick. Oscar clears his throat. "Can I help you?"

"I hope so, Bing. This a local boy?"

He holds up an album, *The Living Dream Sings*. On the cover is Billy's smiling face.

* * * * *

The wind is blowing hard tonight in the outskirts of Sulphur Springs, blowing leaves and debris across a forlorn parking lot, rocking a sign reading, "Motor Park. $2 a night." The place never does much business, and in the winter months it's nearly deserted, with only a handful of year-rounders scattered over the lot.

Candles burn in the windows of the battered Vagabond trailer parked in space #5. That's where the party is. Billy sits on a love seat, guitar in his lap, staring at a coffee table covered with magazines. Cheap dime store magazines. Detective rags.

The pale echo of some kids playing kick-the-can be heard just barely over the brand-new disc playing on the turntable.

'Give it up,' cries the lawman.
'And tell me your tale.
Tell me what you did to Dear Lyla.'
And her lover sings, 'oh no.'

Billy strums along, sings low and sad. "Oh noooo."

On the cover of a magazine, a pretty blonde crouches in the shadow of a looming bad man. She raises her splayed fingers in front of her face. Billy pushes it away. "Reminds me of a gal I used to know," he says to no one in particular.

Dark, dark water closes over him. He smells disease and death. The waters from the lake, from the basement...

"This is bad," he says.

And no one is listening. Not the hulking pinhead with the childish face. Not the chain-smoking transsexual with her caked-on make-up. Not the two strippers sporting complementary black eyes.

'Make your peace,' begs the chaplain.
'Please, please,
where can we find Dear Lyla?'
And her lover sings, 'oh no.'

"Oh nooooo."

Dick opens his black doctor's bag and begins arranging its contents on the table. Spike dances around and mimes something that Billy can only assume is a demented impression of a nurse.

Doctor Dick preps a stainless-steel needle. Nurse Spike assists, cracking open a glass vial. The glittering instrument is mesmerizing.

'Say your prayers,' says the hangman.
'You're about to take a trip,
a trip to see your Dear Lyla.'
And her lover sings...

Billy whispers. "Oh no."

Dick holds up the needle. "Ready?"

"Give it to me, Dick!"

"Don't worry, Billy baby. Uncle Dick will oblige."

The dope slides home into Billy's vein.

Dear Lyla, Dear Lyla,
I miss you, Dear Lyla,
I did you wrong,
but I write this song for you...

Billy leans back as the dope rushes through his body. Dick smiles. "This shit is so fucking wild, Billy. It's like, you can step outside yourself. You get up and walk across the room, turn around and look at yourself."

Billy does just that. He sees the child/man giving the transsexual a tattoo, Spike unzipping Dick's fly.

"I love fucking on it. You know what it's like, Billy? It's like watching someone else fucking, like in front of a mirror, only different."

Billy feels the blonde stripper's fingers on his belt. She winks a mascara-heavy eyelash. "You ready, rock star?"

"No thanks. I have to be going." The dope hits his brain with a crash and suddenly Billy can't stop talking. "I have a very bad feeling about this place. It reminds me of the summer house we stayed at for the weekend. In Bakersfield. The place was inhabited by the spirits of dead women." He gives her a serious look. "Just like this one."

"Honey. I was just going to give you a blow job, not a lobotomy." She staggers into the bathroom. The transsexual wears a Halloween mask of the devil. Lost in her own world, she dances with a whiskey bottle. Dick and Spike are nodding out.

Candles burn on the windowsill. Billy grabs the vials and the syringe and shoves them in his pocket. He opens the window. A gust of wind. The candles burn brighter.

Billy drops hard on the gravel outside, stumbles into the darkness.

On the sill, the candles jump and ignite the curtains. No one notices or no one cares.

As fun as the game has been so far, with the can clamoring up and down the street, a wind burnt kid in a fluttering windbreaker is ready for something new. So when he smells smoke, he's off at a run, stopping only when he comes face to face with a man with ash in his hair, and a guitar slung over his back.

"Mister, what's happening over there?"

The thudding of the kid's racing heartbeat makes it hard to tell if he can actually hear people screaming. The flames rising from the burning trailer crest around Billy's head.

"Someone," he stammers, "someone should help them."

"How about you, mister?"

Billy stares at his legs, willing them to move. "I...I..." The dope makes him wobble. The evil wind tosses the echoes of a scream around the lot. Billy's legs give way, and he drops on his knees, hands digging into the dirt. "It's..." He coughs. "It's just the loons."

"The what?"

"The loons." The thought gives him strength. "Help me, boy. Help me up."

The boy struggles to help him to his feet. Billy gives him a crooked smile and tussles his hair. "Yeah, those are the loons from down on the river flats."

"If you say so, mister."

"Sometimes they go on like that all night. You can't sleep or anything. They just get louder if you try."

* * * * *

Twisted undergrowth fills every empty space in this part of Sulphur Springs, every unplanted yard, every forgotten meridian or street divider. When the scrub brush packs it in and the gravestones take over, you know right where you are. Where all roads end.

Billy weaves between the headstones, stumbling over the ankle-high grave markers. He pulls an artificial flower from a cheap vase. He sticks it in his lapel, which cracks him up. He whistles, which cracks him up some more.

He stands over his father's grave.

RYAN CLOVER.

White lights flash in Billy's eyes. He looks around for headlights, but it's all in his head.

"Here you are, you old bastard! You never got nowhere, did'ja Dad? Not like me! I brought down the house at the Riverside

Rancho every time I played. I played with Jimmy Wakely, Spade, Tex Williams, the Texas Playboys, Sons of the Pioneers, all the greats! Chuck Barry, Ray Charles – these guys opened for *me*! Eight albums. Three movies. Toured in thirty-eight of our great states. When you finally croaked, I played the Hollywood Bowl that night. The Bowl, you shit! I raised a bottle for you that night and told the whole audience, 'My Daddy's dead. He never did a kind thing in his life. All he ever wanted was one thing - to get the hell out of Sulphur Springs. But he never did.' And here you are! You're still here!"

Billy hacks and spits at the headstone, but it only ends up on his shirt. He wants to piss on the grave, but that isn't going to happen either.

He hears something. A rustling somewhere nearby. Like a fluttering of giant wings above him.

"Is that your fucking Angel, Dad?" Billy spins an awkward 360. "The one who's come to take me home." His eyes wildly search the darkness. He tries to light a smoke. Cigarettes scatter over his boots. "Well, I'm ready for you, Angel baby! Let's go. Let's go now!"

Billy's laugh turns into a choking sound and then a weak gasp. He slides down the gravestone. His eyes are searching but they aren't finding anything. The sound in his ears is the river, rushing wild, tossing him, now he's underwater, everything's muted. The streetlights go out, one by one.

Chapter 10

Treat Me Nice

The first day of Billy's new life begins with pain. He lifts himself from a mound of earth, stiff all over. His head aches and his vision is blurred. He spots a path out of the graveyard and stumbles that way, lost and disoriented.

After a while, he comes to some train tracks and follows them until they lead to a liquor store. There's an idling truck and a guy tossing a stack of newspapers onto the sidewalk.

The first thing that really sticks with Billy is the headline.

Sulphur Springs 10¢

Bulletin

Deadly Fire Kills Seven

Singer Billy Clover Feared Among Dead

Police arived at the scene of a deadly fire at the Mayberry Motor Park. The origin of the blaze is unknown as are the names of the seven dead found at the site, however one are thought to be Billy Clover. Clover was born in Sulphur Springs and had fame as a rock and roll singer. **More information to come...**

Stunned, Billy rips a paper from the stack. A storekeeper breaks his reverie. "Hey you jerk! What do you think this is? A library? Give me a nickel for that goddamn paper!"

Billy tosses a coin at the storekeeper and whistles as he walks away with the first purchase of his new life. Being dead might just be the best thing that could happen to him.

Chapter 11

Mystery Train

A half-a-world away, the 3rd platoon crouches in the jungle. The jungles in Vietnam are a scary place at night, especially with a full moon casting shadows.

These guys are new in country. You can tell by their uniforms, still relatively clean, not stiff with months of dried sweat, or stained with the multiple colors of awful that the jungle has to offer. The newbies who think they're tough lean against rocks, chewing, spitting chaw. The rest fidget on their heels, shifting their weight, M-13s clutched hard.

"I gotta piss," one spits out. He's been holding it for a long time. His pale face looks ghostly white against the many shades of jungle green.

"Don't disappear," chuckles one of the toughs. He sports a heard-it-all countenance, but his fresh crew-cut belies his act.

"I'm not going to disappear, just piss."

"You sure?" pipes up another. "Lots of holes out there. Lots of tunnels."

"Yeah, and booby traps."

"Tigers. Bears."

The rest guffaw.

"Sometimes things do disappear," comes a voice from the shadows. All faces turn towards the man crouching there. Eternal stumble. Alert but haunted eyes.

"You talking about Johnny Casio, Sarge?"

3rd platoon loses Sergeants like crazy. After a year in country, Tom is the last man standing among the original members of his company. His promotion is so new that the brass hasn't issued his third stripe. Or maybe they don't think he'll last long enough to stitch it on. He nods, scrapping mud from his boots with the barrel of his rifle.

"That true?"

"I was there."

"The rest of the platoon saw it?"

"We all saw it."

The tough chimes in. "Kid, that platoon is all dead. Except for Sarge here."

"I'm the only one left to tell the story."

"What's the story, Sarge? This guy got blowed up? Like Elvis?"

Tom lights a smoke, cupping his hand over the glowing tip. "This kid from Maryland. Johnny Casio. During a firefight, a tunnel rat's grenade went off right beneath Johnny. I saw it happen. I saw it explode. One second Johnny was there, next second he wasn't. Finally, the enemy retreated, and we picked up what we could from our dead. Their tags and whatnot. But Johnny's body was gone. No blood, no bones, nothing. It was like he just vanished." He lets out a long, long stream of smoke. "It was like a dream."

"Maybe the Vietnamese carried him away during the shooting?"

Tom's eyes turn a shade of crazy. "You listening? There was no blood. No pieces of his uniform. Absolutely no trace. But," he leaned in closer, "that's not even the craziest part. Six days later, we got EVACed halfway across the country, Bien Hoa, just north of Saigon. We're moving through the jungle, and I think I hear something, something in the sky. It was clear skies that day. I look up and don't see a thing. But I still hear it. Like this real low moan, coming from way up. And then we see him. Johnny."

"What?"

"He fell out of the sky. Right out of the clouds. We watched him, all the way down. Landed right in front of our squad." Tom climbs to his feet, cracking his back. "Like I said, some people don't just disappear."

The crew sits silently, eyes wide.

"Let's head out," Tom says.

Chapter 12

Don't Be Cruel

"Hang on, boss." Sport feeds another dime into the payphone outside the post office. A sun-faded sign hangs in the window – an astronaut on the moon, 10 cents. "They aren't confirming much, but the guy was seen leaving the tavern with two fruits. Seen by who? Half the drunks in Sulphur Springs." He snarls at an old farmer waiting outside the booth. "When the cops pulled the bodies out of that trailer they were sizzling. Burnt dark as midnight."

"You don't need to lay on the relish, Sport."

"What's that boss? I can't hear you."

Marcus gets loud, "I'm saying you don't gotta be so cheery about it. The guy used to be a friend of mine."

"Who? This jerk Clover?"

"You don't know him. Back in the day, before he hit big, he was a swell kid. A little twisted but we all are."

"You crying, boss?"

"Screw you, Sport."

"All I'm saying is that you paid me to find him and to do what needed to be done. Well, done is done, and believe me, these fools are well-done."

"I appreciate your tact." Marcus sighs. "Ok, get your ass down here."

The farmer knocks on the glass. Sport yawns. "I'll be back in town on Monday. See you then, boss."

Sport rips the receiver from the phone. He shows it to the farmer with a laugh. The old man just shakes his head and wanders back to his truck.

"Fucking hicks." Sport jumps in his convertible and hits the accelerator pedal, blowing out of this town at 80 miles per hour.

He cruises past an old cemetery. Sport leans on the gas and the Corvair picks up more speed. Ahead, a sign reads "Los Angeles, 275 miles." He checks the rearview window. "Well, I'll be damned." He hits the brakes, squealing to a stop in a cloud of burning tire rubber. He throws the car in reverse.

Billy finishes urinating on the signpost as the Corvair backs up next to him. He zips up. "Keep driving, fella."

Sport rolls down the window. "I ain't looking for that kind of action, Slim."

"Beat it, man. I ain't holding either."

"That's for sure, Billy boy. Burning up a trailer full of hustlers and freaks. That's some company you keep. I knew you was more than just a good ol' country boy."

"I ain't who you think I am. Name's Dale." Billy starts walking.

"Bullshit, Clover." Sport keeps pace in the Corvair. "You like being dead, huh? What are you pulling here, Clover? Insurance scam?"

"Like I said, my name is Dale."

"Ah cut it, Billy. I heard your fucking record, man. I heard that song you wrote. 'Dear Lyla.' Are you fucking crazy? That song is basically a confession."

"I don't get you, sir."

"Jesus, you're a real character. Don't take me for some hillbilly hick. I'm from Hollywood. I've seen your movies, man. I know who you are."

"Do you?"

"Yeah, I do, Billy. I work for Marcus Rydell."

Billy picks up the pace. "Doesn't ring a bell."

"He owns a club you frequent. He also owns a gal you frequent. This stripper, real looker, name of Lyla. She disappears, along with his 1962 Burgundy Continental. Mister Rydell is a man who cares about his property, so he has me looking around. Her roommate thinks she may have gone up north. The motor mouth tells me that Lyla has a thing for a famous singer. 'Any idea where he comes from?' I ask. She says, 'Sulphur Springs'. So I drive up here and go to the first tavern I can find and what do I hear on the jukebox? A little number by a local boy, called 'Dear Lyla.' Very catchy stuff, Billy."

"What can I say?" Billy shrugs. "It's a gift."

"That cat, Oscar? He played me some more of your new material. You're one loony son of a bitch."

"Oscar doesn't understand the artist. He just understands bank statements."

"Personally, I hate this kind of music. I'm a jazz man. Stan Getz, Art Pepper, Chet Baker. That's music, boy."

"Well, it seems we have different musical tastes. I'll be on my way then, unless you want a fucking autograph."

"Shit, Clover, you are a real rube. Do the math some time. This gal had looks and talent. She brings in a good three hundred bucks a night. For Mr. Rydell, this bitch was a printing press for hundred-dollar bills and now she's disappeared someplace." Sport scoffs, "I can't believe the guy is all choked up over you. Sobbing in a little hankie right now, I betcha?"

Billy stops dead in his tracks. Takes a few steps. Stops again. Turns on Sport. "You think Rydell has it tough? You know what I see at night? Her dead face! I can't stop it. So put a bullet through my brain, pal. You'll be doing me a favor, you slick ass fucker."

The car pulls to a sudden stop. "Goddamn, Clover!" Sport laughs and shakes his head. "You are one messed up number."

Billy is quiet now. "You haven't even scratched the surface."

"I'll bet. Jesus." Sport sizes up the cowboy. Billy matches him pound for pound, inch for inch. But Sport figures he could take him in a fight. Easy. He pushes open the passenger door. "I need a drink."

Billy hesitates, then. "Shit. Me too."

*   *   *   *   *

This roadside bar is a couple of miles over the county line. One might expect it to be dark, since the majority of its clientele are hookers who've seen better days and men who are happy to believe that they're getting more for their buck. "The Tender Trap" doesn't confound expectations.

For some reason he cannot figure, the darkness doesn't suit Billy. He moves his drink to the edge of the corner table, closer to the light of the jukebox.

Well people walk by and they stop and stare,
they giggle and they stickle at the clothes I wear.
It's just another day like it always goes,
when you're hangin' around on Skid Row.

"Who's this, Slick?"

"A fella out of Bakersfield. Merle Haggard."

"What you call it? Country or rock?"

"A little of both."

"Like I said, I ain't much into this shit, but I understand it. It's like the blues. It all comes from the heart. That's why when I heard your Lyla number, I knew it had to be true." He lifts his drink. "Here's to absent friends, may they always be standing on the right side of the tracks when the train comes through."

"I like that. You got style. What's your name?"

"Alvin, but you can call me Sport."

"You probably can't see me, but I'm sweating here, Sport. Not cuz of what you and Marcus are going to do to me, but because of what's going on inside me. Something's broken."

"Broken where?"

Billy points a shaky finger at this head. "Here. Where my songs come from."

"I'm just a fan. You're the artist. Fill me in."

"I used to get off on performing. Put me on a stage and I'd stay up there until they turned off the lights or I passed out from exhaustion. Then it was all about the ladies – same thing, go go go, completely lost in it. And all about the fame..."

"The big time, huh?"

"Yeah, the big time. But now..." He pauses to light a cigarette. "Now, all that's left is the songs. They're in there. And they want out."

"So how do you handle it?"

"I got a new friend, name of Miss Morphine."

"I can see how that might be a good remedy for sleepless nights and voices from the grave and all that. But what happened to you and this gal? Lyla."

"You got her picture?"

Sport produces a photo. Lyla poses pretty, her face glowing red from the light of Billy's cigarette.

Billy taps the photo. "You see that mug? She was a dreamer. Came to Hollywood like most of the pretty girls, stepping off a bus at the station right there at Selma and Vine. Fresh and sweet. And, after three years and all the bad times she'd been through, she was still a dreamer. She still believed."

"Kind of hard to imagine."

"Wild huh? Even wilder? She got me believing. Believing I had different songs in me. You see, I never worked on a chain gang or danced in blue suede shoes or twisted with some fucking twins. Or cared much about the colors of the flag. I can only write about that crap once, after that, it's just pure speculation."

"Write what you know, huh?"

"And when I tried it, really tried, I figured something out. Something that scared me."

"What did you find?"

"Something dark. Dark deep inside." He catches his breath. "It scared Lyla too."

"So you killed her?"

"No!" Billy is crying. "I didn't kill her. But I killed her spirit. Her dreams. Us, living the happy Hollywood life, in a happy Hollywood house with twin beds and comfy armchairs. God, it was heartbreaking – her face after those dreams left her. I'd do anything for her. What could I do?"

"What did you do?"

"I tried to ease the pain. When she asked me where I went when everything else was gone, I showed her. I showed her my little kit and my friend, Miss Morphine."

"And...?"

"We were out by the pool. I made up a couple of needles. One big dose for me, a smaller one for her. Before I could stop her, she took them both. Just plunged them one after another into her vein. Closed her eyes."

"And...?"

"Dropped into the water. By the time I pulled her out..." Billy waves one hand slowly across the table. "I buried her in the Caddie. In the river where I used to fish as a kid."

Sport pushes his chair back from the table, laughing. "Man, you just blow my mind!" He claps his hands. "Billy Clover, folks! Last of the Singing Cowboys!"

Billy wipes his teary face, takes a little bow. A hooker hovers over them, flashing an eyeful of wrinkled flesh. "You boys in the mood for a tumble. I'll give ya a two-for-one. Call it a Family Discount?"

Sport flashes some bright white teeth. "What are you talking about, honey?"

"If you two ain't brothers, what are you? Lovers?"

Billy shows her a knife. She just laughs. "Yeah, that's it. A couple of queers who like screwing someone the same size and shape. Maybe share each other's shirts and pants, wear each other's shoes. That turn you on?"

She storms off, her knee-high cheap synthetic boots clacking on the file floor. Sport fishes some ice from his drink and tosses it at her back. "Don't go away mad, baby, just go far, far away."

Billy dries his tear wet face. He laughs. "Boy, I like how you talk. How'd you learn to talk like that?"

Sport eyes a knife in Billy's hand. He opens his jacket and gives Billy a peak of his .38. Billy slides the knife to him. Sport smiles. "I like you, Billy."

"When you going to kill me?'

"Aw that? I'm going to give you a pass."

"Honest? What about Rydell?"

"Far as he knows, you burned up in that fire."

"Billy Clover died in that fire, but I don't feel any different."

"Change your name, become someone else. Start over, maybe that will set stuff straight."

"I'm all screwed up, Sport."

"That's your advantage, Slick."

"I don't get you."

"If you're as nuts as you say you are, well, maybe you can trick yourself into becoming a new person. Forget all those things that haunt Billy Clover and start over."

"Take someone else's name, personality, memories, habits. Their life."

"Something like that." Sport looks hungry. "You still got that morphine?"

Billy nods. "Doesn't seem like your style."

"Art Pepper. Bud Howell. Che Baker. Now Billy Clover. I gotta give it a go. You know somewhere that we can get right?"

*   *   *   *   *

They step into the parking lot. Billy spots a pay phone.

"Gimme a minute."

Sport walks towards his car. "Just a minute, kid. I'm hungry."

Billy drops a bunch of change in the phone. "Hey, Walter, that you?"

"That you, Billy?"

"It's me."

"It's late, Billy. I'm tired."

"It's just this one thing, Walter. You remember we were in that Durango Kid film and we were the band in a saloon. There was shoot-out and The Durango Kid jumped up on the stage with us and shot all the bad guys. At the end, Johnny Marker... you remember, Johnny right?"

"Sure thing, little guy. Kid got spooked whenever the camera rolled."

"That's him. And when Durango finished shooting he spun his silver guns and said, 'that's a big guitar there.' And Johnny was supposed to play a little riff then faint, you know, fall over. He couldn't do it. Take after take. Everyone was pissed. He just couldn't do it."

"You stepped in and did it. You never played a bass in your life."

"Good night, Walter."

"You are a good guy, Billy."

"I was."

Sport honks from his convertible.

*   *   *   *   *

A busted neon sign features a prospector swinging a pick into the Vacancy sign. The words "The 49er" buzzes above in bright red neon, blinking off and on sporadically.

Inside room 107, Sport runs his eyes over the collection of objects laid out in front of him. The needle, the vial, the belt. They comprise his entire world, as his eyes dance across them. The needle, the vial, the belt.

What goes unseen, then, are the black and white images of Jackie Gleason cavorting in *The Life of Riley*. Also, the dirty hotel room. The worn couch and the tattered blinds.

Billy's hands move and each item, in turn, leaves the coffee table, only to return. The needle, the vial, the belt. "You know Marcus was a drummer?"

"Rydell? No shit."

"Terrible drummer. Those guys with no rhythm always end up in business end of things." He slides the needle into Sport's arm and presses the plunger home.

Sport feels the dope course slowly through his body, leaving a certain numbness in its wake. "You want to see something?" His hands loose as eels, Sport digs in his pocket and comes up with a wallet. He fumbles out a photo.

Billy unfolds it and stares at the black and white. "Who is he?"

"That there is the late, great Elvis Presley." His face is grey and sunken, crewcut hair flat and as lifeless as his corpse. He lies on a silver gurney, a sheet covering his lower body and missing arms. "I know a guy who knows Fukazaki. He's the LA County coroner. He got me this a few years back."

"You think this was how he really looked?" The corpse's eyes are closed. "Like before he woke up in the morning?"

"If he's sleeping, he's having a hell of a bad dream."

"That's really him."

"That's him. No make-up or fancy gel."

"Wow. Dead Elvis."

"Man, this shit feels thick. It feels like mud pumping through my veins. Warm mud." Sport empties his lungs with a long sigh. "You know, I used to be a fan. When I was a kid. Loved his movies, his look. The way the girls went wild. You were pretty cool, too, when you were young. No offense."

"None taken."

"I tried to look like him. Talk like him. That hair. Black as black. I thought somehow his cool looks and easy ways would give me a life filled with dames and hot rods. Wasn't as easy as I thought."

"Believe me, I know what you're talking about."

"How'd you pull it off? All those years? Being the new Elvis?"

"Easy. I didn't."

"Man, this stuff is *warm*."

"You hear that? The loons down on the riverbank. That's what they sound like."

It's Billy's turn. His hands move again. The needle, the vial, the belt.

"I don't hear nuthin'."

Billy lays the works back on the table. The needle, the vial, the belt, the hammer.

"You want to see something?"

In the parking lot, Billy fumbles around under the dashboard of a rusty Thunderbird, no wheels, up on blocks.

Sport supports himself with one hand on the ripped vinyl soft top. "Whose car is this?"

"My brother's. I gave it to him."

"You're a prince."

Billy pops the trunk. The hotel's neon sign blinks off.

"What's this?"

"Billy's hiding place."

Sport peers into the trunk. Too dark to see. The neon light blinks back on. Billy's behind him. "I don't see anything."

The light blinks off. Sport stares into the darkness.

"Billy?"

Chapter 13

It's Now or Never

Mama finds her way to the door just before the second knock. The stranger outside still has his hand raised when she opens it.

"Yes?"

The man smacks gum and sucks on a toothpick. He's very tan and very blond, smart looking in his racing jacket. "I'm sorry to bother you, ma'am. I'm looking for Mrs. Clover."

"I'm her. You another reporter?"

"You getting many of them?"

"Some."

"There are bound to be more, lots more. But I ain't one of them. ma'am, my condolences to you."

Mama chokes on a sob. "Thank you."

"I was an acquaintance of your son Billy, ma'am. I knew him from Hollywood. We were both part of society there, very close. When you're successful like your son was, you can never be sure who you can trust. I was devastated when I heard of his death, as were others in our elite circle. So much promise and talent in a man that young."

"Thank you, sir. It is such a shock and I miss him dearly. I'm sorry, but I didn't get your name."

"My closest friends, especially dear old Billy, they call me Sport."

"Sport." Mama squints, peering at the man. Squinting has never improved her eyesight before, and it doesn't now, so she cannot see that the blond hair is bright blond, too blond, and the tan is inconsistent and greasy.

"Yes, ma'am. I had to get up here when I heard the news. See, before Billy died in that fire, I happened to talk to him by telephone. He seemed a little down. He felt he was failing in his music and was misunderstood. He was thinking of coming back to Hollywood and giving it another shot. He didn't want to leave though, until he made amends with his dear mother."

"Amends?"

"He felt that he let you down somewhere along the way. He felt he wasn't the son you wanted him to be. He wanted you to know that he was sorry. Sorry for everything."

"That poor boy. He didn't have to be sorry for anything. I loved him no matter what. There's something about your first born. Even if he hadn't been a successful singer, I would have loved him. He was very misunderstood."

"Well, I just thought you should know he was sorry. He also wanted to tell you he forgives his brother. Donny is it?"

"That's his younger brother. He didn't understand Billy."

"Well, he wanted to tell you he forgives Donny for being so mean to him and telling fibs about how badly he was misbehaving and what not." The strange man starts for his car.

"Donny should be home any minute now. You can tell him yourself."

"I'd like to, ma'am. But I must be hitting the road. It's a 'long haul', as you folks might say, back to the city. They need me back there, back in Hollywood."

He pops the trunk on the Corvair. A shapeless burlap sack sags next to his guitar. Billy smiles and lifts something out of the bag. A decapitated head. He brushes the blond hair from Sport's lifeless eyes.

"If I'm going to be someone else, I might as well be you." Billy whispers, and carefully wraps the head in burlap and closes the trunk.

"Well, thank you again, young man," calls Mama from the front porch. "Drive careful."

"I will, ma'am. Good day to you."

*   *   *   *   *

Highway Patrolman Jones scratches his ear, wondering where they all come from. In the daily completion of his duties, he passes over this bridge twice a day and he's never once seen another car in the area. But now that it's a crime scene, the carloads of lookie-loos and gawkers stretches a hundred yards down the road.

"Move along, folks. Nothin' to see here."

Of course, there is plenty to see. Two policemen in a rowboat toss lines into the murky water, dragging the river bottom. A tow truck hauls a big purple car from the water, filthy with mud.

"Hey Copper, what's going on?"

"What did you just call me?"

The driver stares at him from behind dark sunglasses. His hair is bleached blond. His dark tan is shiny and weird. "Are the fish jumping or what?"

"Lose the attitude, pal. And get a move on before you cause an accident."

The Corvair accelerates away. The patrolman spots the Sheriff climbing the embankment up from the river. "You see that clown?"

A sunburnt Sheriff removes his peaked hat and mops his sweaty brow. "You radio the fire department like I asked you?"

"Yeah Sheriff, ten minutes ago." He motions at the scene below. "That thing looks pretty ripe. You think them dainty firemen are going to let it mess up their shiny red engines?"

The sheriff studies the water-logged corpse in the car. The remnants of a flowered dress cling to her shape. "I don't know, Jones. Maybe she can ride in your cruiser, right up front with you."

The road curves around the edges of a small, still lake. Billy has one hand on the steering wheel while the other does double duty, juggling the bottle and the cigarette.

A road sign reads "Bakersfield -9 miles. Los Angeles - 126 miles."

A couple of boys have their poles in the water. The shadow of Billy's car passes over them, and one boy waves lazily. The car turns off the two-lane blacktop onto a dusty dirt road, past untended fields.

The sun is setting behind a two-story farmhouse as Billy pulls up. He flips on his headlights, illuminating the faded words written in cracked red paint across the door, "Murdering Bastard!" The windows of the first floor are covered with plywood and graffiti. "Killer!" "Rest in Hell!" No one bothered with the second floor, except to paint "Fuck You!"

Billy climbs from his car. "Just like I remember it. Fuck you too!"

Inside, there's plenty of beer cans and trash, and more graffiti. Billy finds his favorite in the upstairs bedroom. "Eat Shit Murderer!" This seems as good a place as any to shoot up.

The sky is burning red. Billy finishes his business and stumbles to the window. He stares down at an overgrown orchard behind the house. Slipping down the walls, he hears a faint sound. It grows and grows. It's a woman screaming.

"Billy? Are you awake? Did you hear that?"

"I heard it, Donny, go back to sleep."

"I wish Daddy were here. I'm scared."

"He'll be here tomorrow, Mama says."

"There it was again! That's a scream, Billy."

"No it wasn't. It was one of those loons from down on the lake. Like Mama said. Go to sleep."

"It sounded like a lady screaming."

"Just go to sleep."

Donny can't sleep and Billy can't sit still. He climbs over his brother's cot and tiptoes down the stairs. His mother is sleeping in the living room. Beyond that is the kitchen. And beyond that, the basement door.

The sound of a slow drip greets Billy as he creeps down into the basement. His feet touch water.

He stares into the darkness below him. And descends.

There's a sound coming from behind a closed door, deep in the basement. Billy walks through the ankle-deep water. He passes a work bench, tools scattered around. His eyes fix on a hammer, dripping blood.

Muffled sounds behind the door. Billy reaches out a shaky hand and touches it. He gives it a soft push.

A naked man covered in grey hair leans over a table. He turns to Billy, revealing burning eyes and a disembodied woman's body on the table.

He smiles, showing big yellow teeth. And he winks.

* * * * *

The old shopkeeper greets the first customer of the day. "Howdy, Hank."

Hank rolls his eyes. "Get a load of what's behind me."

Billy steps inside. His tan is freshly reapplied, and shoe polish stains his hands. "What happened to the loons? They migrate?"

The two men at the counter share a look. Hank decides to field this one. "They don't migrate. They stay all year round."

Billy grabs a pack of Lucky Strikes off the counter, breaks the seal and lights one up. "Billy has heard those calls in the middle of the night since that summer. But last night? Oh, Billy slept good last night."

Now it's the storekeeper's turn. "You been here before? I don't believe I recall you."

"Daddy Clover sure tricked us good. He sent us here for a little vacation, said he'd be down soon. 'Cept he never figured to show up or for us to come back neither."

"I don't follow you, mister."

"It was a set-up. Dad sent us here for one reason. The old geezer who lived in that house was supposed to add us to his private collection, dig? The one he keeps in his cellar, dig? 'Cept Billy told Mama some scary stories about what he saw down there." He blows some smoke. "You know that song 'Cabin By The Lake?'" They nod, dubious. "What a joke, huh? Billy knows the score."

"Yeah? And is Billy gonna pay for that pack of smokes?"

"Sure, Slick. You can call me Sport and Sport can dig it. Gonna get a pop too, if that's okay with you, Dad."

"In the cooler there."

Billy pops the top and wipes the foam onto the floor.

"That's a buck ten, pal. And I ain't got no matches for you."

"You see that out there? In the back seat of that Corvair?"

"The guitar?"

"Yeah. How much would you pay for that?"

"Nothing. Mister, I ain't got no use for it."

"Well, Sport ain't got no use for it either."

"You still owe me a buck ten."

"I get your drift, Pops." He tosses some coins on the counter. "Stay thin, Cappy." He drips cola all the way out the door.

"Jesus Christ, weirdos are just gettin' weirder these days."

The Corvair pulls out of the lot, leaving a thin cloud of dust and an old guitar sitting on the ice machine.

* * * * *

More crowd control. Any more and Patrolman Jones will have

to list it as part of his job description. His girl Mary has been on him about finding different work so it's something to think about. "Move along. Move along."

A kid pushing ten pleads with him. "Come on, Mister. Let me see it, okay?"

"Just run along there." The boys crowding the entrance to the alley clear out when the ambulance arrives, and the patrolman gets his first glimpse of the head. "Well, ain't that the shit."

The coroner calls him over. "What?"

"Nothing. Thought I recognized him."

"Go ahead." He steps aside so Jones can get a better look.

"Looks a little like this goofball I reprimanded the other day at Farrell's Landing. When we were pulling the car out of the river."

"This him?"

"I dunno…maybe blonder…." He motions at the coroner's sunglasses. "Mind if borrow those for a second?" The coroner shrugs and hands over his dark glasses. Patrolman Jones kneels and fits them snugly over the corpse's eyes.

The Sheriff steps up. "What the hell did you go and do that for?!"

Jones starts, standing straight. "Sorry sir. The guy had on sunglasses."

The coroner jumps in. "So, is it him?!"

* * * * *

In a rest stop midway over The Grapevine, the hard climb over the hills before the quick descent into Los Angeles, a little boy in a cowboy outfit jumps from a station wagon. His dad pops the hood, glares at the steaming radiator. "Can I go see the horsies, Daddy?"

Dad grunts and the little boy sprints across the concrete towards the horse trailer. The horses stir restlessly as their owner fills their water troughs. From behind him comes a rough voice shouting, "Alright partner! Draw!"

The little boy spins, his cap guns up and firing. The blond man clutches his heart and dies in slow motion. He smiles and gives the kid a wink. "You like horses, huh? Those are stallions right there. Real studs."

"Really? That's neat, mister."

"You're a real dude in your cowboy hat and chaps there. Let me see that mask of yours. I want to look at it real close."

The kid hands over his Lone Ranger mask, thrilled that an adult is talking to him.

"Okay, Kemo Sabe. Sport's going to hold on to this, okay?" Billy walks off. The kid stares after him. Holsters his guns with a sigh.

Billy passes the truck. A sign painted on the door reads *Fat Jones' Hollywood Picture Animals.* "These gee-gees look ready for a little hey-hey."

The driver looks up, confused. "What'd you say?"

"You taking 'em down to Hollywood?"

"Sure am."

Billy climbs into the Corvair. "That's where I'm headed."

* * * * *

The Hollywood freeway. The Vine Street Exit, next to the Capitol Building. Three blocks north to Franklin. Two block east to Gower. The Mediterranean style apartment complex there. There's a pool out back. You can't see it from the street, but Billy knows it's there.

He smiles. Fate and a well-placed swing of a hammer have led him back to Hollywood. Back where, he now understands, he belongs.

South now. Past a billboard for *Speedway* with Tommy Sands

looking tired in a yellow racing suit. Down past Hollywood Boulevard. Down past Melrose. Down where it's quiet at night and little bungalows line the streets. That's where the address on Sport's license takes him. Patrol cars are parked out front, and cops are coming and going through the front door.

Billy keeps driving.

East. A long way East. Past downtown. Past the railroads. This is skid row. There's a rundown office building there. There's also a payphone. Billy makes a call.

"Artistic Pictures Modeling Agency."

"Put the boss on. Tell him it's urgent."

A pause and then a grunt. "Rydell here."

"Hey, Slick. How you been?"

"Who is this?"

"Sport, Daddy-o."

"I thought you were going to get a hold of me on Monday. What's up?"

"I got your boy Clover."

"Clover? What you pulling here?"

"Nothing, boss. I was mistaken in my previous presumptions."

"What in the hell are you talking about?"

"That Billy is one slippery fella. He faked his death. Right after I talked to you, who should I run into but the clever bastard himself."

"Really, so where is Clover now?"

"I got him. I want extra dough for him though. I want ten grand. Today."

Laughter over the receiver. "Are you kidding me? You must have Kentucky fried your brain up there in Hicksville, Sport."

"Look Pops, I ain't kidding around here. He was a big star. There's going to be a funeral bigger than Elvis'. Gals are gonna wear black all over the country. Half-flags and all that."

"He was a punk. All washed up."

"They called him 'The Living Dream.'"

"I don't know what the fuck you're jiving on about, Sport. When you come down off of whatever the hell you're on, we'll talk. On Monday. Like we agreed. You know I don't do business like this." Click. He hangs up.

"Well, you do now, asshole." Billy jumps in the Corvair and drives into an alley directly across the street. Brakes squeal and horns honk. The alley is full of cars. Billy parks behind a trash container and tosses down some bennies.

A loud knock on the car window and a bellowing voice, "Where's your money? You know you pay like everyone else." Billy stares at the dwarf in the western shirt and cowboy hat.

"You the valet?"

"Why are you giving me grief, Sport? You know the rules. You ain't here for the show, you park out on the street."

"I'm an associate of Mr. Rydell."

"It's Rydell's rule, pal."

"Oh yeah. I guess I forgot. I've been here a hundred times."

"Cough it up. We don't have a problem, do we?"

The bennies are kicking in, so his hands seem like a blur as they pick up the little man and tosses him inside the trash container. "You know what, Slick? We do have a problem." He jams his switchblade into the man's body, over and over and over.

He wipes his blade on the lifeless man's slacks. Slicks back his hair. And heads inside.

Marcus Rydell leans back in his chair and sighs. He misses the old days. After he gave up the nightclub, his life was smooth as silk. His hair even grew back. Temperamental singers, junked-out musicians, he'd had enough of it all. No more payrolls, no more pay-outs. Gone were the headaches over liquor licenses and building codes and all that. The place was a money pit!

Eight or nine years ago, he started Artistic Pictures Modeling Agency with a staff of exactly one, him. He did it all. He cruised Hollywood Boulevard for the runaways and the starving starlets. He brought them here, to this tiny office with the logo of crossed paintbrushes on the door. He broke them in. He collected the money and dealt out the punishment when they misbehaved. Later, he took the pictures and even stuffed the glossies in the envelopes. Just him, a desk, a chair and a couch.

Heaven.

Now, the room is packed with two more desks and two big men. And that's just the muscle. He's got a ticket taker and a projectionist working downstairs. Plus outside contractors like film crews and developers. And then there's the whole print end of the business, the junkie magazine editor and the pervert printer. Plus the inevitable acquisitions of a life of crime – stolen goods and tentacles of illegal activity into a dozen legit businesses. A pawn shop. A strip club. He prides himself on being a sort of "hands off" style of boss, but management issues do arise from time to time. Somebody gets popped, or strung-out, or pregnant, and it falls on him to sort it out.

He's bald now.

Which is why he's always valued a guy like Sport. You tell him what you need and he either does it or he doesn't, and you either pay him or don't. He's independent. You don't even have to shake his hand. Sure, he has his problems, an undue enthusiasm for certain aspects of his work, but in general he keeps himself in check. And he looks cool.

And now he's standing there, chewing gum like a madman, and

looking like a greasy blonde freak in an undersized black mask.

"What the fuck is wrong with you?"

"Nothin', pops. Could use a trim, that's all. I been thinking, though, I may just go long. Real crazy man. Grow it down to my ass and die it purple. That'll freak you out, eh Slick?"

"Freaking me out now, you crazy son-of-a-bitch. What's with the mask?"

"Yippy-yi-ah! I'm the Lone Ranger. I'm the Durango Kid! Ya get me?!"

"No, I don't. I don't get you at all." Marcus kicks the chair of the big man sitting next to him. The thug jumps up and his partner follows him. "Malcolm, Butch, you guys heard me tell Alvin that I'd talk to him on Monday."

"I'm ready to wheel and deal right now, baby. I got your boy out in my trunk. Lyla is dead, you have been avenged."

"That's really you, Sport? I got to say, I barely recognize you."

"He don't look right, Boss." Russell leans closer, reaching out his hand towards the mask. Billy swats it away.

"Country air will change a man."

Marcus has to laugh. "You are a piece of work, Sport. Tell you what, dickhead. Why don't you get yourself a girl, do your thing. I'm showing your favorite loop downstairs. Why don't you go take a look? I know you can't get enough of that shit."

"Yeah, Sport." Butch crosses his huge arms. "Go get some popcorn, get your nut. You should take a shower too; you're looking pretty sweaty."

"Now look, I'm offering you a hell of a deal here. Let's go take a look at what I got." And Billy walks out the door.

Russell has his opinion. "That guy has lost it, boss." Butch counters. "Sport has always been a nut, but at least he has style. He keeps himself composed and sharp. That there is somebody else."

As usual, they disagree. And, as usual, the decision is Marcus' to make. "I've always wondered if the day would come when Sport would fall apart and blow it. Let's humor this asshole. Today just may be that day."

By the time they get outside, Billy already has the trunk open. "Over here, fellas."

Marcus scans the alley. "Russell, find out where Cowboy went. He needs to be watching this fucking lot. Otherwise we're going to have grand central station here."

"He might have just gone around the corner for a pop."

"Find him and tell him to get back and stay the fuck put. I'm paying that freak to watch this lot."

"I'll find him."

"I tell you, man." Marcus sighs, "This business of keeping up with all you guys is getting old."

"I hear you there, Boss." Billy gestures to the trunk. "Check it out." He grabs a handful of bloody shirt and hefts the headless corpse onto the pavement.

"Jesus Christ!" Butch's eyes bulge. "Driving around with a hacked up stiff in the trunk. You drive down from Sulphur Springs like that?"

"Well, he might have attracted a little bit of attention if I let him ride up front."

Marcus kicks some trash over the body. "I suppose you got the head in there too?"

"Naw, I destroyed the head. Knocked out all the teeth. You know, in case of dental records. Chucked the teeth in the river. I fed the rest of it to some wild pigs along the way. Yeah, real tidy."

"Wild pigs?"

Butch scoffs. "Pigs ain't gonna eat meat."

"These do. Wild boars. They ate up all the evidence. I couldn't risk anyone finding out it was him. Clover's real big, a big star, maybe the biggest. But you can see the body. Clover's paid his debt to you. Now, you and me need to get even. 10 grand should do it."

"What the hell happened to you up there? Just look at yourself. It's 1969, man. I'll tell you what. You get in that car, take that fucking corpse with you and get the hell out of Los Angeles and I won't kill you. Then we're even. Go check yourself into a nuthouse, Sport."

"Why would I do that?" Billy laughs. "I was thinking I'd get my money, get a big sandwich, and hit the beach."

Marcus growls. "Butch, you still keep that pistol on you?"

It turns out Butch does. He keeps it in his belt, so it's not too difficult for Billy to grab it. Firing it is even easier. One, two, right in Butch's gut.

"You crazy bastard!" Marcus makes a break. Billy runs after him, firing wildly. Marcus hits an alley door and collapses inside. Billy steps over his body, slipping on the blood. He goes down hard.

When he climbs back to his feet, Russell is waiting in the doorway. His first bullet misses but the second one tears into Billy's neck. Billy falls down the stairs into the basement.

Russell shouts after him, "Die down there, you sick fuck!" And he runs out of the alley.

In the dark corridor at the bottom of the stairs, Billy leans against the filthy wall. He stumbles in the near dark, his hands pressed to his bleeding neck.

He pushes aside some heavy curtains. A movie is playing in the room beyond. A dozen men are scattered around on folding chairs, hands in their laps, staring at the stained screen.

Billy has never been a real movie buff. He can barely stand to watch his own pictures. But this is a different kind of movie. The gals aren't Rita Hayworth or Audrey Hepburn, and the leading man isn't Cary Grant in a sharp suit. In fact, he's naked. In fact, he's Sport.

The movie is poorly exposed. It's blurred and scratched. But that's clearly Sport in that hotel room, lounging on the bed with two naked gals. He tickles the skinny one, her mascara streaked with dried tears. The heavy one drinks from a bottle and lets him fondle her breasts.

Billy fumbles off his cowboy mask as Sport puts on his dark sunglasses. So does the heavy one. She's his favorite gal. Sport has an ice pick. His favorite gal has a butcher knife. They stab and stab at the skinny girl. Now they're kissing. They're smearing blood all over each other and laughing like crazy. They kiss some more and Sport starts stabbing his favorite gal. He's jabbing her in the back over and over. He's still laughing.

One of the perverts sees Billy, sees the blood coloring his shirt. He runs out. A transvestite sees Billy too. "It's the guy from the loop! It's him! From the movie!"

The whole room turns to look at Billy. He just stands there teetering and bleeding. Then he shoots the transvestite in the head.

That's when the sirens start wailing outside and when everyone starts running.

Everyone but Billy. He just stares at the screen.

* * * * *

The first patrol car on the scene is busy with the bodies in the alley. That means the policemen in Car 108 are the first ones down the stairs.

Guns drawn; they enter the dark theater. Chairs are toppled

and the screen is ripped. The room reeks of old sweat and urine. There's a new smell, cordite. And something else.

"Is that kerosene?"

They carefully enter the hallway. A workman's closet door hangs open. Inside, Billy stands, sloshing liquid from a can onto the floor.

"Drop the gun, buddy!"

"I stopped the voices for Billy. Now the visions are haunting Sport. Is there no end?" He tosses a cigarette into the puddles at his feet.

The resulting fireball is terrible. So are Billy's screams.

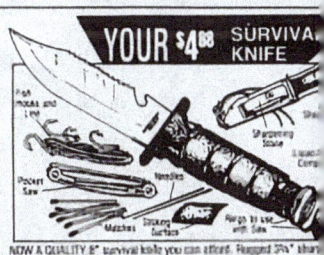

Chapter 14

Burning Love

Wind is blowing cold off Lake Champlain. But it's not the wind that makes Cutey hurry down the dark streets of Burlington.

She ducks into the Crooked Bridge —the only bar open after midnight in this small town in Vermont. She sidles up to the bar and orders herself something sour. It's cash only. She gives the bartender a $20—the smallest bill she has—and turns to watch the band.

They're playing something low and slow with a story to it. The guitar is doing most of the talking. Cutey can't see who's playing that guitar. She moves closer to the stage. There he is, in the back, nearly hidden in the shadow of the speakers.

He's tall and bearded with hair down to his shoulders. His fingers walk up and down the fret, telling the half-empty room what he knows about sorrow.

Cutey smiles. Her thin frame sways to the beat. She likes how he sounds. How he leads the three other men past the crescendo, nodding to the rhythm section when he's ready for the climax.

Cutey claps long and loud. The guitarist gives her a grateful smile as the band takes a break. Half the room is staring at her – the male half. Their dates throw daggers. Cutey is a looker.

Cutey ignores the looks and asks the bartender for a round of whatever the guitarist usually drinks.

"TJ? He's a whiskey man."

"A whiskey then. Top shelf. What else do you know about him besides his drink of choice?"

"When he's not up there making that jazz box sing, he's digging graves. 'Nother for you too?"

She finds TJ sitting alone in the corner. He's reapplying super-glue to some callouses.

"Battle wounds?" she says, sitting across from him. She slides the whiskey over and hits him with her best bedroom eyes. Gold hoop earrings dangle off the sides of her perfect face. Her paisley dress is tight.

"Sorry?" TJ says.

"Your callouses. From playing guitar, I meant. Battle wounds."

"Oh, yeah, I'm a little out of practice. The callouses open back up."

"That was you playing *out* of practice? I'll have to hear you warmed up sometime, goddamn."

Moving closer over the table, Cutey decides he's handsome under that beard. She can see his bright green eyes but also the heavy bags hanging under them.

"Thank you for the drink."

"Well, I'm hoping to get you liquored up and shanghaied for some shows I got booked out west. We could use a guitar player with real talent backing up our bands. Who knows, it goes well, maybe we could cut some tracks. Get you paid. You ever recorded?"

"I'm sorry, ma'am, but who are you?"

"Cutey."

"Thank you, but again, who are you?"

"That's my name. Cutey. And I'm offering you an opportunity. I never heard a guitar cry like that, baby."

"What'd you see me play? One song? Don't mess with me, lady."

She reaches a hand over the table and places it on his. "No fooling, honey. I'm the real deal. Based out of LA." Cutey reaches into her purse and fishes out a folded-up newspaper clipping. She hands it to TJ. He unfolds a black and white photo of her in a mini skirt. An old man in a suit shakes her hand in front of the Capital Records building. The caption reads:

"Artie Bronstein of Capital Records signs Cutey Parker. She's the singer with that Ol' Familiar Feeling."

"My hair's a little frizzy in that photo, but that's me, baby. This cool east coast weather's much better for the 'do." She pats her silky dark hair. "That's when I was still a singer. Now I manage. I'm out here scouting. Talent out west has gotten stagnant. I'm hunting for new blood."

"You see these wrinkles? I'm old blood, lady. Keep hunting."

"Let me get you another drink." She motions to the bartender – another round. "You ever heard of Timmy Redfield And The Red Riders? Jimmy Jack And The Marbles? Rudy Ray And The Comets?" TJ shakes his head. She lights a cigarette. "Of course you haven't. One-hit wonders. Light on 'hit' and lighter on 'wonders'. A cute lead singer out front. We back the airplay on the single, trot him out on the road for six to eight months, then dump him. But the band. The band moves on to the next group."

"'And The', that me?"

She blows smoke. "It's a racket but it beats digging graves."

"I teach meditation on Mondays too," TJ says. "Make tea for a yoga studio now and then."

"Holistic, I can dig that. But I can offer you more. I can get you some exposure."

TJ laughs a mirthless laugh. "That's exactly what I don't need."

"Well, how about this. You hook up with me, let me get you in a studio with a few professionals –"

Cutey's eyes grow wide, looking over TJ's shoulder. He turns and sees a large man, standing by the door, his thick neck turning, scanning the crowd.

Cutey grabs his hand. "This place got a backdoor?"

"How serious is this?"

"Serious."

* * * * *

Outside the club, an even bigger man is watching the exit. TJ wheels a speaker case out the back door, the rest of his equipment piled on top. He opens the back of his van.

"Mind giving me a hand?" TJ says to him. "She's heavy."

The man scans the empty alley, shrugs. They lift the case into the van. TJ closes the door.

"Thanks."

A few blocks away, he pulls over and climbs in back. He opens the case.

"'She's heavy?'" Cutey unfolds herself from the case.

"We're lucky Otis brought his stack tonight. I'll have to get this case back to him pronto. The old man's sensitive about his speakers."

"You aren't going to ask me who that was?"

"No. Everybody's got a reason to get lost."

"What's the TJ stand for?"

"The J is John, my grandfather's name."

"And T?"

"Tom."

Cutey leans over and kisses him. "Nice to meet you, Tom." After a pause, he kisses her back.

* * * * *

Tom lights the last candle on the stone steps of the mausoleum and blows out the match. It's his favorite corner of the cemetery, dominated by a massive birch tree. The roots run thick and deep, so the surrounding graves are all above ground. They make for nice benches.

He puts his jacket around Cutey's shoulders. She notices patches crudely sewn on the sleeves — a sword on a multi-colored shield, another reading 'Ninth Infantry Vietnam.' She wriggles with satisfaction, like a swaddled baby. "This is a helluva place for a first date."

"I'm the groundskeeper and it's a one-man business. No one will bother us." He starts messing around on his acoustic guitar.

"Play me something."

"I usually only play for money."

"We can work out payment later," she says with a wink.

Tom strums a few slow chords. Middle of the road emotionally. Sad but poppy.

"That sounds familiar," Cutey says. "What was that?"

"Elvis. 'I Want You, I Need You.' "

"Subtle."

"You're not a fan?"

"I didn't mind him exploding, I'll leave it at that."

Tom continues to fool around with the melody —changing it up, making it something new. "Some say he didn't. That he arranged it with the Army to fake his death. Now he's living out in the Midwest somewheres, raising cattle. Planning a comeback."

"And you believe that?"

Tom strums some more. Creating as they talk. "Guy like Elvis, you just figure he'll be around forever. Maybe I just like believing that."

"Nobody's around forever. Especially in the music industry. Remember Jimmy And or Tommy And? No. They disappeared. And when Elvis kicked the bucket, that made room for lots of new nobodies. Like..."

"Like Billy Clover." Tom segues into "Cabin By The Lake."

"Then he disappeared too."

"Too bad. His last album was something else."

Cutey laughs. "Don't tell me you're one of those. Those fans of *Songs from the Murder House*."

"'Dear Lyla' was the theme song of Air Calvary. We'd blast that song before they dropped us in the jungle. You'd spend the next week with it running full tilt through your head."

He strums and sings,

'Say your prayers,' says the hangman.
'You're about to take a trip,
a trip to see your Dear Lyla.'

"What a weird left turn that was. He goes from Western Swing to Rock to Country to...that."

"Makes you wonder what was next."

Cutey shrugs. "We'll never know. He's gone."

"Maybe. Some things come back." Tom clears his throat and sings,

"Have you seen young Johnny,
he was part of the 7th Infantry,
with me, oh, with me . . .

chased Vietcong,
through the grasses so long,
now he's gone, now he's gone, he's gone . . .

it was one hot night, the moon shining bright,
when the gunfire flashed, grenades flew,
goodbye Johnny, goodbye friend, goodbye . . . "

"Now this one I know I've never heard before."

"Something I've been piecing together. About this thing that happened back in 'Nam. Can't get it out of my head."

Cutey gets lost in the melody. Sways back and forth on the cold ground. She looks around. The skeletal trees and the tombstones. On top of a hill overlooking it all, a three-story building. A tall Victorian number with a high-pitched roof and a sole window.

"That must have some view," she says.

"It's an old mansion. Used to belong to the people who owned this land. You can see the whole cemetery from up there."

A slow smile spreads across her face. "The whole place."

*　*　*　*　*

Tom climbs out of the backhoe and cracks his back. The sun is down but he's still got more to do. The work is nonstop now that the spring warmth has thawed the hard earth. A backlog of bodies that have been on ice all winter need to be put in the ground.

He counts the new holes. Ten of them, scattered over the cemetery, most of them near the southern wall. Sunday is a big day for funerals. He makes a mental note to make a wake-up call to Glen and the rest of the college kids he's got working over spring break. They need to get in early to lay out the green shrouds around the empty graves and assemble the structures over the open graves where the pallbearers will lay the coffins.

Tom rubs his jaw. He's not used to the clean shave. That was Cutey's idea. She's got a way of getting him to do things. Like open up. He's talked more in last three weeks than in the last three years. He even told her about Alvin. Not much. Just that Alvin was the reason he was laying low, the reason he slept with a gun under his pillow. He knows Alvin won't stop looking for him until he dies or until Alvin dies. If that's even possible...

In turn, she told him about her father. Not much either. Said he was a jerk. That he was famous. And about her ex. He was also a jerk and famous. "Real famous," she whispered, her cigarette shaking between her fingers, ash everywhere. Tom didn't push it.

He sees Cutey in the window at the top of the old house. She worked something out with the owner, renting the place for a steal, using her record producer wiles.

Things are good. They take slow drives around the cemetery on the John Deere mower. Tom drives with his feet, strumming his guitar, Cutey's arms around his waist. She's finally stopped talking about him touring with her bands. Last thing he needs. Jesus. Two tours in 'Nam and exile here in the wasteland. How hard is it to get lost?

He's been secretly hanging little light bulbs all over the cemetery – in trees, behind gravestones, around the tops of mausoleums. He's going to surprise her on her birthday next Friday. The place will light up like a Christmas tree.

He likes that she watches him work. He waves.

Cutey waves back. She's got a nice comfy set up in her nook in the attic. Chair pulled up close to the window. A glass of wine at her side. An ashtray and a full pack of cigarettes. Ready for the show.

The phone rings downstairs. Probably her father. He has a way of finding her. Not that she had made it very hard.

She sweet-talked the organizer of the spring festival at the county fair into giving Tom a solo on the stage, just a few songs. She also arranged for the local paper's cameraman to get a shot of her kissing him under the Ferris wheel.

That's all it took. All her life, the Colonel had fluctuated from not noticing she was in the room to needing to know her every move when she was out of it. He'd been like that since she was little. Since Elvis died.

All his plans and schemes exploded on that field in Germany. The last thirteen years have been spent trying to raise the dead – to find another superstar to take the King's place. She'd seen the boys come and go, all contenders reaching for the crown. Her father would drive them on, preaching like a holy man consumed by the Spirit. He had just one sermon and it was Keep Rock and Roll Alive.

"I gave the world what it needed. Elvis." She had it memorized at this point. "Some say he was a star. He was bigger. He was the sun that all planets circle round. The world has gone off its axis since he passed. Nothing's the same. You've seen it. Good folks turning bad. Winners becoming losers." His voice would swell here. "If you listen to me, and follow what I say, you can rise that high. You can never lose. Just don't forget the two Rs..."

This dream, this obsession, was not spared on his family. He married a pretty girl with an okay voice, sure he could mold her into a hero for the Cause. After she disappointed, topping out at 47 on the billboard charts, he lost interest. She killed herself a few months after Cutey was born.

Next it was Cutey's turn. She didn't like to sing, didn't like to perform. But it didn't matter. Gotta keep that music alive.

Her one and only album failed to chart.

The ringing downstairs doesn't stop. Insistent. Maybe it's her husband. She can picture him – hand gripping the phone tight, dressed, as always, to the nines, casino style, maybe a freshly pressed cashmere suit and silk tie, his famous face radiating vicious intent.

After the better part of a decade making bad decisions, the Colonel ended up in hock to the wrong people. This big shot knew wrong people. With a nod from the boys in Chicago, this big shot cleared up the Colonel's problems. Next thing you know, big shot is his partner.

He is also her husband.

She fell hard. He was twenty-seven years her senior, but he knew how to lay on the charm. And he was the only man the Colonel was afraid of. That meant a lot.

But the spell faded quickly. He was a kind man to Cutey, but he was a bloodthirsty son of a bitch to anybody who looked at her. It was jealousy of biblical proportions.

Cutey sits upright. A long black car slowly creeps along the cemetery walls, headlights off. It parks by the ornate dark metal gate. Unmoving. Engine idling.

Their divorce was all the thing for a couple of months. Her face on all the rags in the supermarket racks. He was cordial to her, but the homicidal jealousy persisted.

Cutey couldn't figure out why, but she got a kick out of it. Flirting with random men, then hearing about how her ex's bodyguards took them apart. It was scary at first, but it was a rush.

She always picked musicians. Nobodies. Playing for the love of it. Untarnished by the business. She felt, in a way she couldn't understand, that she was protecting them, keeping them from the Colonel and his Cause, his crusade for Rock and Roll.

And that heightened the thrill, the rush.

But, after a while, the rush dissipated. The problem was she never got to see it happen. Just got to listen to the greatest hits tape recounted by the ex in late night calls. Always second hand—until now.

The newspaper photo was a week old. Plenty of time.

The phone rattles away. Let it ring. She's not going anywhere. She pours another glass of wine.

Tom checks his watch. Almost midnight. One last chore. He moves among the graves, distributing the gold-plated hand shovels that the widow, daughter, whatever-next-of-kin, will use to dump the first bit of dirt into the grave. Glen and his dummies always forgot this. He places a shovel on top of a newly planted gravestone, noting, not for the first time, its surprising weight. He guesses the weight adds to the gravity of the solemn ritual.

Cutey leans towards the window. She can make out two shadows crossing over the top of a far hill, making their way down towards Tom. These two look big and tall. Her ex-husband is waiting in the dark somewhere; he'd put on some weight since his younger days but she knew she would spot him.

"Showtime," she whispers to herself.

"Hey pal, you in charge of this joint?"

Tom is surprised to find that he is not alone. "You could say that."

"'Cuz it looks like you're missing some guests." The laughing guy points to the empty graves. He reminds Tom of a gunner named Rally back in Vietnam. He had the same busted up mug and gaping mouth hole. He'd been a bully and thought he was real funny, a real cut-up. Taking this cue, Tom plays it like he played it with Rally. Friendly and folksy.

"You got me there. You fellas lost out here?"

"I guess we are."

Tom starts to raise his hand to point at the entrance when the other man grabs it and twists it behind his back. Quick moves for a giant.

"We got him, boss."

Cutey sees a figure swagger from the shadows. Her heartbeat quickens. It's the ex.

"So this is the latest cutie-pie?" The man pushes back the brim of his fedora, illuminating his face. "Howdy fella," he says with bitter sarcasm.

Tom just stares. Cutey said her ex was famous, but...

"What you want us to do with him, Mr. Sinatra?" says the giant.

"Hold him tight. I wanna get a close look at this peach." Frank Sinatra leans close to Tom. "Aw, he ain't that cute." He spits in Tom's face.

His boys laugh. "Yeah, a real mess, boss."

"It's the nose. His nose is crooked." Frank works some brass knuckles onto his fingers. "Let me see if I can fix that for you."

Tom tosses the golden shovel into his face. A lucky shot, it splits Frank's nose wide open. It happens so quickly and unexpectedly that Tom is able to shove the giant behind him, twist free and sprint into the graveyard.

Patrick, the Rally-lookalike, pulls his gun, scanning the area. "Where'd he go?!"

"He's in one of the graves!" Ol' Blue Eyes clutches his bleeding nose between two jeweled fingers. "Shoot that cocksucker, Patrick."

The ground surrounding them is full of empty graves. Tom is nowhere to be seen. The pair of goons head out, guns up and ready. Jeremy, who could be Patrick's brother, reaches a grave, takes a breath, then lurches forward, gun pointing into the darkness of the hole in the earth.

Lights go up all over the graveyard. Jeremy spins. Tiny lights dance in the wind wherever he looks. Like a giant Christmas tree.

"Psst." Patrick nods towards lights swinging under a tree branch. "Over here."

A shovel swings out of a grave, catching Jeremy in the shin. He screams and collapses, his gun firing.

Jeremy's stray bullet lands straight in Patrick's chest and the giant pitches backwards, blood gushing.

Tom scurries from the grave. Jeremy fires twice. Tom disappears into the darkness beyond the lights.

"Fucking schmuck," Frank shouts. His fancy tie and shirt are covered with blood. "I'm gonna kill him. I'm gonna fucking kill him. Get up. Get up, Jeremy." He grabs his bodyguard by the jacket and lifts him up. Jeremy whimpers, "I think he broke my goddamn knee."

"Shut up. Go that way, around that fucking machine. I'm gonna follow these trees. We'll snare him in."

"Patrick's bleeding pretty bad, boss."

"Get his gun!"

Jeremy kneels beside his partner and pries the blood-spattered gun from his hand. Patrick feebly reaches out to him A bloody gurgle sounds like "help."

"I'm sorry. The boss says. You know..."

A gun in both hands, Jeremy limps to the backhoe. He peers around the large tire. Spots a small field of open graves surrounded by birch trees. He makes his way to the first tree. No sign of him. He moves towards the second tree.

Tom leaps from the tree, landing on Jeremy. Jeremy hits the ground hard, stunned. He makes a low moaning sound. Tom punches him in the face until he doesn't make that sound anymore.

Cutey leans out of the window now, straining to see. The phone rings. She jumps.

She starts down the stairs. Tom is shy, but he comes out of his shell once a guitar is in his hand, or they are under the covers. Something deep and bad happened to him.

Why is she thinking about Tom?

He cries out in his sleep. Sweating buckets. Cutey holds him, calms him, stokes his hair. It feels nice.

She realizes that she is running down the stairs, taking them two at a time.

She's panting when she grabs the receiver.

"Good evening, is this Cutey Parker?" a woman's nervous voice.

"What? Yes, who is this?"

"My name's Abbie. I'm a nurse at St. Thomas Hospital, here in Las Vegas. I'm sorry to be the one to tell you this, but your father's had a stroke."

"The Colonel?"

"Mr. Parker, yes. He's in the ICU here. You're listed as his next of kin."

"Is he . . . what's it look like?"

"It was a large stroke. Lots of pressure on his brain stem. If he does regain consciousness, he may be paralyzed for life. Now if you would like to make arrangements . . ."

Cutey only hears the rushing blood in her ears. He's done for. The Colonel will never recover. The crusade is over. Rock and Roll is dead.

The rest is nonsense now.

She drops the phone and, barefoot, runs out of the front door. Out into the cemetery.

There's no sign of Tom. She runs past the backhoe and trips over Jeremy, his face a pulp of blood and bone. Then she hears her ex-husband's million-dollar voice, somewhere in the dark.

"That you, tulip? Where's your new plaything? You come to watch him bleed."

"Frank, don't. Baby, please. There's no need for this now."

Frank steps from behind a mausoleum, picking up Jeremy's gun as he does. "That right? How about that clown in St. Louis. And the crooner over in Atlantic City. There no need for that, tulip?"

"Frank—"

Behind her ex, Tom slowly creeps forward with a pickaxe in

hand. Frank sees the glance from Cutey and swings his gun arm around. The pickaxe swings wide, catching nothing but air. Frank fires.

Tom is hit in the shoulder. In pain, he drops the pickaxe and takes a desperate lunge at Frank with his good arm. Sinatra dodges with ease, stepping aside like a matador with a charging bull, giving Tom a slug to the back as he falls into the dirt at Frank's feet.

Tom finds a knee and raises his head and sees one thing. A silver .32 revolver pointed directly at his face. Frank chuckles, "party's over."

Time slows down for Tom. Staring into the hole that will soon vomit out the bullet which will end his life, Tom's brain goes into overdrive. A million thoughts at once.

What came was anger. Rage! He wanted to spew fury at Sinatra. His lousy songs on the last dozen albums, crap covers that the man believes he can own by his famous voice and nothing else, selling out the greatness that once was, a joke. Cruddy movies, petty beefs with old friends, younger and younger girlfriends with big dreams of nasty divorces.

And what of *his* life? How has Tom lived? Two words attacked him. "In fear." Fear has dominated his life for as long as he can re-member. Ever since that field in Eldon Corners, he's had a psycho on a revenge trip dogging his heels. Add to it, there's the countless Viet Cong who tried to kill him, so many comrades' dead in so many exotic ways – impaled on bamboo stalks, hastily amputated by a bouncing Betty, snake bites, a salvo of bullets from an unseen foe. He'd lived through all that. But *this*? This is his death? Killed by Frank fucking Sinatra.

And not even The Voice. Not "Strangers In The Night" Sinatra. Not "From Here to Eternity"Sinatra.

The Sinatra pointing a gun in his face just starred in *Dirty Dingus*

Magee. He just recorded "It's Not Easy Being Green" – covering a fucking Muppet!

All the rage disappears, leaving him empty. Helpless. He lowers his head.

"I wanted to be a poet."

"You want to lay some on me, chump?"

"Can death be sleep,
while life is but a dream,
and scenes of bliss pass as
a phantom by?"

"I hate to say it, kid, but that's crap. Utter crap."

Frank pulls the hammer back. The click echoes in Tom's ears, and he suddenly finds himself leaping at Sinatra. This go-around the fallen icon doesn't move in time, and Tom piles into him, knocking Frank to the ground. The older man is surprisingly strong. Tom will never win with one arm. He scans the ground for something to use. Anything to give him an advantage. No rocks, no tools. Nothing.

He improvises, bending his knees and pivoting, twisting his body while maintaining a tight grip on Frank. He grunts and swings Frank towards the nearest open grave. Frank isn't expecting the ground to just end like that and falls into the grave with a loud "Fuck!"

Tom starts for Cutey. They have a little time before Frank is out of the grave and back at him. He knows what to do. He'll grab Cutey and they'll run for his car. Get the hell out of here. Hit the road and just keep going.

He stops mid-step.

Alvin. Last time he ran from a fight, he ran all the way to

Vietnam. How far would he have to run this time?

"Dear Lyla, Dear Lyla, I've got more songs to sing..."

He strips off his belt and wraps it over his knuckles. Cutey grabs his arm. "Tom...I love you..."

Tom dives into the grave.

Cutey jumps with each grunt and curse and hard blow below. She inches closer to the lip of the grave. And then silence.

"T-Tom?"

A bloody hand rises from the grave. Then another. Tom lifts himself clumsily from the grave, rolling on his back. His face is a Jackson Pollack of blood.

Cutey clutches him tight. Tom gasps in pain but he's okay.

"Is he...?"

"He won't be bothering you anymore."

She has to see. She creeps towards the grave. Steeling herself, she peeks inside. She gags. "I guess people can disappear, if you hit them hard enough."

Tom drags Jeremy's corpse past her and tosses him into the grave. It lands with a thud.

"When they lower the coffin tomorrow, there will be three more bodies in that grave. But no one will know." Tom tosses her a key fob. "You in?"

Cutey doesn't miss a beat. "Completely."

"Drive his car as far you can. Leave it somewhere no one will find for a good long time."

Tom staggers on his feet. Cutey grabs him in a tight embrace.

"You know what, Cutey?"

"What?"

"I think I figured out the last line to my song."

Billboard HOT

THIS WEEK	LAST WEEK	WEEKS ON CHART	TITLE — Artist (Producer) Label, Number (Distributing Label)		THIS WEEK	LAST WEEK	WEEKS ON CHART	TITLE — Artist (Producer)
1	1	11	**WHERE'S JOHNNY** — Tom Starr and the Singing Marines (Cutey Parker), A&M 1505 — WBM		34	18	11	**CALL ME (Come Bac...** — Al Green (Willie Mitchell), Hi ...
2	4	9	**THE CISCO KID ●** — War (Jerry Goldstein, Lonnie Jordan & Howard Scott for Far Out Productions), United Artists 163 — B-3		35	36	7	**CHERRY CHERRY (Fr... August Night")** — Neil Diamond (Tom Catalano),
3	3	10	**SING** — Carpenters (Richard & Karen Carpenter), A&M 1413 — WBM		36	62	3	**MY LOVE** — Paul McCartney & Wings (Gra...
4	2	12	**THE NIGHT THE LIGHTS WENT OUT IN GEORGIA** — Vicki Lawrence (Snuff Garrett), Bell 45-303 — SGC		37	43	8	**ARMED AND EXTREM...** — First Choice (Stan and Harris &... Philly Groove 175 (Bell)
5	7	15	**LITTLE WILLY** — The Sweet (Phil Wainman for New Productions Ltd.), Bell 45-251 — WBM		38	41	9	**I'M DOING FINE NOW** — New York City (Thom Bell), Chelsea 78-0113 (RCA)
6	11	7	**YOU ARE THE SUNSHINE OF MY LIFE** — Stevie Wonder (Stevie Wonder), Tamla 54232 (Motown) — WCP		39	21	14	**SPACE ODDITY** — David Bowie (Gus Dudgeon), R...
7	8	10	**MASTERPIECE** — Temptations (Norman Whitfield), Gordy 7126 (Motown) — WCP		40	45	4	**LEAVING ME** — Independents (Art Productions)
8	10	9	**THE TWELFTH OF NEVER** — Donny Osmond (Mike Curb, Don Costa), MGM 14503		41	46	6	**I CAN UNDERSTAND...** — New Birth (Fuqua III Productio... RCA 74-0912
9	13	9	**STUCK IN THE MIDDLE WITH YOU** — Stealers Wheel (Lieber-Stoller), A&M 1416 — WCP		42	47	7	**BLUE SUEDE SHOES** — Johnny Rivers (Johnny Rivers),
10	5	13	**AIN'T NO WOMAN (Like the One I've Got)** — Four Tops (Steve Barri, Dennis Lambert, Brian Potter), Dunhill 4339 — WCP		43	49	6	**PLAYGROUND IN MY...** — Clint Holmes (Paul Vance & Le... Epic 5-10891 (Columbia)
11	15	10	**DRIFT AWAY** — Dobie Gray (Mentor Williams), Decca 33057 (MCA) — NAK		44	60	3	**STEAMROLLER BLUE...** — Elvis Presley, RCA 74-0910
12	6	14	**NEITHER ONE OF US (Wants to be the First to Say Goodbye)** — Gladys Knight & the Pips (Joe Porter), Soul 35098 (Motown) — SGC		45	53	4	**IT SURE TOOK A LON...** — Lobo (Phil Gernhard), Big Tree...
13	12	12	**STIR IT UP** — Johnny Nash (Johnny Nash), Epic 5-10949 (Columbia) — B-3		46	37	11	**STEP BY STEP** — Joe Simon (Raeford Gerald for ... Productions), Spring 133 (Poly...
14	17	13	**PEACEFUL** — Helen Reddy (Tom Catalano), Capitol 3527 — HAN		47	51	6	**LET'S PRETEND** — Raspberries (Jimmy Ienner), Ca...
15	25	8	**FRANKENSTEIN** — Edgar Winter Group (Rick Derringer), Epic 5-10967 (Columbia)		48	48	8	**CINDY INCIDENTALL...** — Faces (Glyn Johns), Warner Bro...
16	19	11	**WALK ON THE WILD SIDE** — Lou Reed (David Bowie), RCA 74-0887 — HAN		49	50	7	**WHO WAS IT?** — Hurricane Smith (Hurricane Smi...
17	20	11	**WILDFLOWER** — Skylark (Eirik the Norwegian), Capitol 3511 — HAN		50	55	5	**HEARTS OF STONE** — Blue Ridge Rangers (John Foge... Fantasy 700
18	9	17	**DANNY'S SONG** — Anne Murray (Brian Ahern), Capitol 3481 — WBM		51	56	10	**TEDDY BEAR SONG** — Barbara Fairchild (Jerry Crutch... Columbia 4-45743
19	22	8	**REELING IN THE YEARS** — Steely Dan (Gary Katz), ABC 11352 — WCP		52	54	7	**I KNEW JESUS (Befo...** — Glen Campbell (Jimmy Bowen),
20	14	14	**KILLING ME SOFTLY WITH HIS SONG ●** — Roberta Flack (Joel Dorn), Atlantic 45-2940 — B-3		53	58	4	**DRINKING WINE SPO...** — Jerry Lee Lewis (Steve Rowlan...
21	24	11	**DAISY A DAY**		54	61	3	**SUPERFLY MEETS SH...** — John & Ernest (Dickie Goodma... Rainy Wednesday 201 (Gulliver...
					55	65	3	**NO MORE MR. NICE...**

NEW YORK QUEST

ONLY 15¢

LATE CITY FINAL

Friday, May 15, 1973 Breezy & Mild & Partly Cloudy 49 / Weather page 30

Sports page 15

PAGES 37-40

In The Wake of the Oscars:
Red Carpet Nightmares

SINATRA STILL MISSING

Family fears Ol' Blue Eyes may be dead

EXCLUSIVE

A grip of fear not paralleled since the infamous Summer of Sam has halted activities around the city. This time with a twist; those who have avoided punishment from our court system could now face the ultimate justice. The latest victim, as with the previous victims has been tried in New York courts and aquitted of all charges on technicalities which seem flimsy at best.

FULL STORY, page 2

NEW YORK POLITICS IN FULL BLOOM: The State Of Our City

page 37

Coda

All Shook Up

The day ward is empty except for two men in wheelchairs.

The Colonel's eyes stare straight ahead. Unable to move his head, he sees only Billy.

Billy is gauzed and bandaged. Tubes feed him and pump him full of medicine. He's paralyzed and he can't move or speak. But he can still feel, and burns hurt. Third degree burns cover 98 percent of his body. He's just waiting to die. If not from skin suffocation, from pain.

The right eye is covered in gauze, so it's impossible to tell if it is open or shut. But the left one is wide open. It darts around in panic.

The loons are gone. But, even through the heavy bandages, Billy can still hear the music. It's still alive in Billy's head.

The Colonel eyes fix on Billy. He sees some small movement in Billy's legs. They are shaking. Pretty soon his whole body is shaking.

Shaking all over.

Acknowledgments

There would be no *All His Damned Mother's Sons* if there were no Josh Lawson. Josh was a unique man, truly one of a kind, a raconteur, filmmaker, actor, writer and the hardest working man I've ever known. At some point before I met him, Josh had written a screed of a screenplay about a washed-up country singer, a pervert and a woman-killer, who only sang Eddie Noack's songs. We played with this character over the years, wondering what to do with him. Then one day, Josh went to the hospital with a backache and died a week later. I could never hope to write a character like Josh, but Billy Clover's genes share some of his biological makeup. When Billy steals the mask from the kid and says, "I'm going to hold on to his, okay?" That's Josh. When Sport tells Marcus he's going to grow his hair long and die it purple to freak him out, Marcus replies, "You're freaking me out now, you crazy son of a bitch." That's Josh. He wrote a dozen treatments or more that should have been made. I'm proud that a piece of who he was is alive in this book.

Thanks go to Patrick Cooper, a madman of his own kind, who kindly lent me his idea of a soldier who disappears while on patrol in Vietnam and falls out of the sky days later. This story not only built out the Tom character in *All His Damned Mother's Sons*, but also inspired the ending with his conflict with Sinatra. Thanks, Patrick!

All my gratitude to my loving wife, Stella, who read the early *weird* drafts; my daughter, Briar, who gives every song I play for her a chance and loves KISS & Elvis; Syd Garon for being a mensch; Scott Kinsey for kicking out fantastic graphics; and, as always, my publisher & editor, Mark Givens. Mark is truly the best a writer could work with. And a great friend.

About the Author

Tim Kirk is the author of the western novella *Burnt* and a collection of short stories *The Feral Boy Who Lives In Griffith Park*. Tim also makes films as writer and director including *Sex Madness Revealed*, *The Miami Vice Incident*, and the award-winning *The Mystery of Durango*. His producing credits include *Room 237* and *The El Duce Tapes*.

AUTHOR PHOTO BY BRIAR KIRK

112 Harvard Ave #65
Claremont, CA 91711 USA

pelekinesis@gmail.com
www.pelekinesis.com

Pelekinesis titles are available through Ingram, Gardners, directly from the
publisher's website, and at your favorite local bookstore.

www.ingramcontent.com/pod-product-compliance
Lightning Source LLC
Chambersburg PA
CBHW050347030726
47503CB00008B/2657